Hawaiian Interlude

Hawaiian Interlude

Dorothy Francis

THORNDIKE
CHIVERS

This Large Print edition is published by Thorndike Press®, Waterville, Maine USA and by BBC Audiobooks, Ltd, Bath, England.

Published in 2004 in the U.S. by arrangement with Maureen Moran Agency.

Published in 2005 in the U.K. by arrangement with the author.

U.S.   Hardcover 0-7862-7156-6   (Candlelight)
U.K.   Hardcover 1-4056-3218-6   (Chivers Large Print)
U.K.   Softcover 1-4056-3219-4   (Camden Large Print)

The text of this Large Print edition is unabridged.
Other aspects of the book may vary from the original edition.

Set in 16 pt. Plantin by Christina S. Huff.

Printed in the United States on permanent paper.

British Library Cataloguing-in-Publication Data available

Library of Congress Cataloging-in-Publication Data

Francis, Dorothy Brenner.
    Hawaiian interlude / Dorothy Francis.
        p.   cm.
    ISBN 0-7862-7156-6 (lg. print : hc : alk. paper)
    1. Hotels — Employees — Fiction.   2. Young women —
Fiction.   3. Hawaii — Fiction.   4. Large type books.
I. Title.
PS3556.R327H39 2004
813'.54—dc22   2004061533

For Richard

Chapter One

Teetering on the scant running board of the swaying cable car, Vicki Foster clutched the brass support shaft as she braced for the shooting descent to the wharf. She murmured an apology as she felt her blue handbag bounce against the ramplike lap of a fat lady lucky enough to have found a seat on this open section of the crowded vehicle; then she smiled at the touch of Greg's protecting arm across her back as he, too, grasped the safety pole.

Like a clattering, lumbering robot, the cable car lurched to a shuddering crawl as it conquered the hilltop, then plunged in a fury of speed and sound. Vicki gasped. The salt air slapped her face and snarled her hair, and cars, trucks, and people dissolved into a miasma of motion. Would they crash in a mangled heap at the foot of the hill?

Vicki turned her head in time to see the handsome Negro operator flash a triumphant smile and throw his weight into a muscle-knotting tug on the black steel hand-brake. The cables groaned, the wheels rasped, the car stopped. A brassy odor clung to Vicki's sweating fingers after she released the metal post, and as if by reflex she wiped her hand down the side of her blue skirt.

Greg thumped to the pavement. "And San Francisco scores another accident-free trip to Fisherman's Wharf." His deep voice throbbed with laughter as he offered Vicki his hand.

"That last hill always chills me." Vicki grinned, tried to swallow the cottony taste that clogged her mouth, and brushed a wisp of blonde hair from her eyes.

"Riding the cable was your idea," Greg said. "Sometimes you act like a tourist in your own home town. I wanted to escort you here in the luxury of my Volkswagen."

As they inched along the crowded sidewalk beside the wharf Vicki welcomed the hustle-bustle that hindered Greg's conversation. She had deliberately chosen this setting for their last evening together, partly from sentiment, but mostly for pragmatic reasons.

Greg had brought her here two years ago on their first date, and she liked the idea of saying good-bye in the same setting; it seemed to round the golden months of their dating into a completed circle. But more important, she wanted to avoid a super-solemn farewell. The roar of the clattery-bang cable car quashed any serious conversation, the wharf's jostling crowds precluded privacy, and the reek rising like a fetid gas from the open vats of live lobsters and boiled crabs discouraged romantic thoughts.

Making the decision had hurt. Greg had suggested the Seal Rock dining room or the Top of the Mark, but her determination to control this situation made her plead for a seafood dinner at Whalers' Cove. Who could propose in this atmosphere!

Vicki sighed. Perhaps she was being featherheaded, or maybe even egotistical, but she was convinced that a girl could tell when a boy was about to suggest marriage, and she felt that it was the girl's choice either to encourage or discourage the question.

Five close friends in her own graduating class had suddenly grown "left-handed" in order to show off pinpoint solitaires, and each had claimed to be *so surprised*. Yet Vicki doubted this. Although she would love an engagement ring, she was determined to dodge making this decision just yet. As long as she pleased her parents by avoiding marriage plans, she knew it would be easier for her to have her own way in other important matters.

"Here we are." Greg opened a white porthole-shaped door, and they entered a crowded restaurant. A green-uniformed waitress whisked them to a handkerchief-size table, splashed ice water into two glasses, and snapped menus before them.

"What would you like?" Greg asked.

Vicki ignored the menu. "Prawns with the usual."

"Make it two." Greg smiled at the waitress. "French fries, iced-tea, tossed salad with Italian dressing, and orange sherbert."

After the waitress left, Greg laughed. "We're true San Franciscans. The thundering Pacific at our doorstep, and we order prawns shipped in from Louisiana."

"Best thing on the menu." Vicki drank in the seafaring atmosphere and inhaled the mouth-watering aroma of frying shrimp. "Don't you just love this place, Greg?"

"What you like, I like," Greg said. "But next week we'll dine in better style."

"I'm leaving tomorrow, Greg." Vicki blurted out the words in spite of all her intentions to mention this news calmly.

"Tomorrow!" Greg's voice boomed like a bass chime, and several diners glanced at him in surprise.

"I've been wanting to tell you," Vicki said, "but I hate sad good-byes. I thought we

10

could sign off with a flourish here at the wharf. After all, three months isn't forever."

"But where are you going?"

"Honolulu," Vicki answered.

Greg scowled. "Honolulu! You're kidding!"

Vicki didn't blame Greg for being upset. This secret had nagged at her until she learned of Greg's debating workshop at Kansas University. Her plans for a summer in Honolulu had seemed less drastic when she realized that Greg's pre-law course was taking him from San Francisco.

"The Fosters are starting a family-exchange plan." Vicki kept her voice feather-light. "My cousin, Sue, and I have misered our baby-sitting coins for years so that we could have a fabulous vacation after high school graduation."

"If you've so much loot hoarded, you'd better apply it to a college education instead of gallivanting off to Hawaii." Greg frowned, and his eyebrows formed a black window of worry across his tanned forehead.

"Save the lecture! The plane fare wouldn't keep me in school even one quarter."

"But, Vicki, you'll have other vacation expenses."

Vicki sipped some water to hide her nervousness, and it felt as heavy as quicksilver as it slid down her parched throat.

"Not many," she said. "You see, I'd planned to help Dad in the flower shop this summer, and Sue had agreed to work in her mother's Honolulu hotel. So we decided to exchange places. This way, we'll each have a home, a job, and a vacation setting. Sue's even planning to enroll in college here next fall."

"Leave it to you to come up with one of your bright ideas!" Greg's tone softened. "Sorry I was so grim, Vicki. You caught me off guard. I've no right to plan your summer, and I really don't begrudge you a vacation in Hawaii if that's what you want. You might even be able to save enough money from your hotel job to pay part of your college expenses. You know that your dad would help you with the rest."

"Oh, Greg!" Vicki paused while the waitress served their plates. For months now, she had tried to tell herself that her high school marks were the bars that caged her desire to go to college. It was a subject she didn't like to discuss with anyone, and especially not with Greg, who had a knack for seeing through shams.

"Let's not argue," Vicki said after the waitress left. "I'm simply not college mate-

12

rial. The universities want straight 'A' brains like you and my brother, Verne. The average student has about as much chance of surviving as a mackerel in a school of blue sharks."

"You're not an average student and you know it," Greg said.

"I've got the 'C's' to prove it." Vicki picked a thread from her napkin.

"The reason you have 'C's' is because you didn't try for anything better," Greg said. "Surely you've noticed how hard Verne had to work for those 'A's.'"

Vicki sighed. She had noticed, all right. And for as long as she could remember, she had heard about Verne's outstanding grades. For a while she had even tried to match his achievements, but no matter how close she came to a perfect report card, Verne always topped her, and their parents invariably compared their daughter unfavorably with their son. If Verne himself had lorded it over her, she could have retaliated. But Verne wasn't that sort. Vicki adored her older brother, and in order to squelch her feelings of resentment and inadequacy, she quit trying to match his scholastic record and began majoring in extracurricular activities. Vicki knew she had gained a well-earned reputation for impulsiveness as she hid her feelings of self-doubt by trying out for everything the school offered.

The ruse had fooled her parents. They quit comparing her scholastically to Verne, and instead, commented on how different their children were turning out to be. Verne paid little attention to outside activities, and Vicki's parents were proud when she was elected class historian and editor of the school paper.

"Well, it's your life," Greg said after Vicki's long silence, "but I can't help feeling that deep down you really want to study art or creative writing. You're making an important decision with a closed mind."

Vicki kept her eyes on her plate. She had always wanted to write children's stories or illustrate children's books. But these were her private dreams; she wasn't ready to share them just yet, not even with Greg.

"College is for the brains," Vicki repeated.

"And what if you're right about being average?" Greg asked. "The world's full of happy, useful, average people who've made something of themselves."

"The world may be brimming with them, but the colleges aren't," Vicki said. "Miss Average is the gal who wings home for good

at the quarter break. But you'll never understand — you've always won top honors."

"Not so." Greg sugared his tea, then
snapped his fingers. "Maybe that's the answer!"

"Afraid I missed the question."

"I made so-so grades until I decided to be
a lawyer," Greg said. "After that, school really took on meaning for me. Maybe if you
set a goal . . ."

"No good, Greg." Vicki wished she could
lose herself in the babbling voices that
flowed about them, or in the liquid melody
of the ballad that poured from the juke box,
but Greg bent forward like a prosecuting attorney, his dark eyes demanding her undivided attention.

"What about your folks, Vicki? They want
you to go on to school."

"Sure they do," Vicki said. "But it's all
they can do to finance Verne's education. I
won't allow them to scrimp for my sake."

"Because if you did, you'd feel obligated
to do your best, wouldn't you?" Greg asked.

Vicki felt as if her skin and bones were a
gossamer veil and that Greg could see
through to her heart. He was right, but he
couldn't seem to understand that her best
academic efforts were never good enough in
the eyes of her parents.

"College isn't for me, Greg. I'll pay my own way through a term of secretarial school, then . . ." Vicki gulped. She had almost blurted, "Then we can be married and I'll work to help you finish law school."

In the back of her mind, Vicki believed that marriage would solve all their problems. She and Greg would have each other, and their love would provide the protective atmosphere in which they both could develop their talents — Greg as a lawyer and she as a writer. A person didn't need a college diploma to write a book. Vicki was determined to master this art on her own, secretly, safe from all critical eyes. But these impulsive thoughts were but fragments from a fanciful mosaic of the far-distant future. She had no intention of mentioning them to Greg now.

"Greg, you will do me a favor, won't you?"

Greg sighed. "Name it." Looking like an attorney who had just lost his case, he frowned.

"Since we've both agreed to date others during this summer's separation, I hope you'll take out my cousin, Sue, once or twice before you leave town. She'll arrive tomorrow night, you know. It'd be awfully nice if you'd introduce her to some of your friends."

"What's with this Sue?" Greg asked. "Can't she manage on her own?"

"You bet she can!" Vicki's words snapped like copper pennies against Formica, then she relaxed. "Of course she'll meet lots of kids this fall when she enrolls at college, but she'll be new in town this summer. Sue's a beauty, Greg. Here, I have a picture with me." Vicki rummaged in her purse. Opening her blue billfold, she offered a colored likeness of Sue for Greg's inspection.

"Not bad!" Greg exclaimed. "Not bad at all. But, of course, I prefer blondes." He gazed fondly at Vicki before glancing back at the snapshot. "Sue has an Oriental look about her eyes, Vicki. Didn't you say you were cousins?"

"Sue's father was Dad's twin." Vicki paused while the waitress removed their plates and served their orange sherbert. "But her mother is Chinese-Hawaiian."

"Seems like a nice mixture." Greg returned the picture. "What does your uncle do in Honolulu?"

"Uncle Tim died in a plane crash several years ago," Vicki said. "He was stationed at Schofield Barracks when he married Aunt Noel. She turned their home into an apartment-hotel after he died, and has

17

supported herself and my three cousins for the past five years."

"Noel," Greg mused. "She sounds like a tropical Christmas carol."

Vicki spooned a bite of sherbert and let the frosty sweetness melt on her tongue. "Not too bad a description at that, but Noel is a shortened version of her real name, Noelani. Her Hawaiian mother named her after a princess — the daughter of some ancient Hawaiian monarch, I've been told. I don't really know my aunt very well."

"How long since you've seen her?"

"Ages." Vicki laid her crumpled napkin on the table and eyed the waiting crowd that bottlenecked the cafe entrance. "Uncle Tim brought his family to San Francisco for a visit about six years ago. Sue and I were twelve then, and we became pen pals. We've written to each other every week since the day we met."

Greg picked up the dinner check. "What about the rest of the family?"

"Sue has two brothers. Mark is twenty and already a graduate of the University of Hawaii, where he was a football star, and Buzz is sixteen and will be a high school sophomore."

Vicki relaxed now that she had told Greg about her long-dreamed-of trip to the islands. How silly to guard such a secret for so many months! But she knew Greg. Given time, he might have talked her out of her plans. She admired his glib arguments and his puncture-proof logic as long as they weren't aimed in her direction. Her only defense was to toss twits about his pre-law lingo whenever he threatened to submerge her with words.

Leaving Whalers' Cove, they wandered into a Far East import house and browsed through narrow aisles, viewing everything from antique Japanese porcelain to modernistic hammered-brass keys from India. The minutes rushed by, but Vicki did her best to ignore the time.

A chill wind knifed the evening as they hopped another rumbling cable car and jolted toward Chinatown, where they strolled through quaint Oriental art stores and incense-scented curio shops until their feet begged for mercy. Later in the evening the cable car was less crowded, and Greg got them a seat in the smoke-filled enclosed cubicle for their jouncing ride to the Fosters' neighborhood.

Vicki felt Greg's warm hand clasp her own chilled fingers as they sauntered up the hill to her parents' apartment.

"I won't come in," Greg said as they

19

reached her doorstep. "Give my regards to your folks, and remember to write to me while you're away."

Greg's sudden kiss stopped her answer; then, before she could laugh, cry, or even speak, Greg disappeared into the chilly night. She was alone. Well, that was what she wanted, wasn't it? Vicki wondered. At times she wasn't sure of anything.

Chapter Two

A night light shone when Vicki stepped inside her living room. How quiet! Of course, with her father away at a florists' convention and Verne off to summer school, she really hadn't expected a fanfare. In fact, she was glad to find that her mother had already retired; there had been such stinging arguments, such paralyzing tension between them for the past grinding months that Vicki welcomed the silence.

Age eighteen must be the most tormenting time in any girl's life, she thought; then she smiled to herself, turned off the lamp, and tiptoed to her bedroom. She had had this same feeling all through her teenage years and she had survived. But being eighteen was scary. When she was younger she had bucked decisions over teeth braces, lipstick, dating, and most other adolescent problems, but her parents always had the last word. Now things were different.

Although Mom and Dad advised, urged, and pleaded, Vicki knew that the lasting judgments — the important verdicts — were now up to her. But she couldn't go her headstrong way ignoring her family's feelings and wishes. That was the tough part. In trying to please herself as well as her parents, she was beginning to feel that her whole life was one strangling compromise.

She was leaving Greg without the security of a diamond on her finger because her mother opposed drawn-out engagements as well as teen-age marriages. But against her parents' wishes, she refused to attend college. Perhaps she had goofed on her decisions, but they were made, and it seemed easier to cling to them than to make new ones. Anyway, she meant to store her problems like a bundle of winter clothing. The islands waited; she envisioned an enchanting vacation. Hidden deep down inside was the unspoken hope that she would return to San Francisco a more mature person — a person who knew her own mind, who could go her own way with the firm conviction that she was doing the right thing, and that the right thing was an early marriage.

In spite of sweeping sadness at the thought of being separated from Greg, and pulsating excitement over her trip to Hawaii, Vicki slept soundly until mid-morning the following day. The hollow silence of the apartment told her that her mother was at the flower shop, so she slipped on her blue robe and wandered to the kitchen for orange juice. It wasn't until she returned to her room to finish her packing that she had to fight the numbing ache in her throat and the stinging tears that burned her eyelids.

Why was leaving home so painful? She wanted to go, she had her parents' consent, her relatives expected her. What was her trouble? She was going to be away for a few weeks — not forever. No. That was wrong. She was leaving for good. Oh, she would come back many times, but family relationships would be different. Never again would she really belong here in this room.

One minute Vicki felt like a soaring kite, then in the next second she half hoped for the tug of a restraining string. Well, she couldn't back out now. She tried to swallow the brown-sock taste in her mouth, determining to hide her feelings behind a mask of casualness. That seemed to be an adult way of doing things.

Her clothes were washed, pressed, and mended, and transferring them from closet to travel bag was a simple chore. But closing the case was another matter; she had to cut down somewhere. Her sketch pad and the battered notebook that housed her daily journal were bulky but essential items. She couldn't leave them behind. After much stuffing and pulling, Vicki removed her blue sneakers and a heavy skirt, shut the bag, and sat on the lid. Juggling up and down like a gymnast, she listened until she heard the chrome catches snick into place.

"Dope!" Vicki stooped and scowled at her mirrored reflection as she buttoned the jacket of her blue cotton suit. "Dopey dope!" All her life she had worn blue. Verne had teased her about being so tall that she blended into the sky, but she shrugged off her brother's jokes because she liked being willowy. She wore blue because it accented her eyes. A plain girl had to point up her best features, and Vicki had considered pale blue her special hallmark, her brand of distinction. How puerile! She frowned at her room: blue walls, blue carpet, blue bedspread — even blue luggage. This blue bit was high-school stuff. As soon as she reached Honolulu, she would buy the brightest muumuu on the islands.

"Vicki!" her mother called from the front doorway. "Are you all packed? It's time we left for the airport."

Vicki hadn't heard her mother come in, but the stringent tone of her usually pleasant voice told Vicki that this upheaval was probably as hard on her mother as it was on herself. Vicki was glad that her father was away. At least that farewell was past.

"Ready for takeoff, Mom." Vicki glanced at her watch, grabbed her bag, cosmetic case, and purse, and struggled into the living room.

"Here, let me help." Although her mother's compact frame and china-fragile looks belied hidden strength and determination, Vicki smiled down at her and allowed her to carry only the small cosmetic case as they left the apartment and hurried toward the Chevrolet in the driveway.

"You have your ticket?" Mrs. Foster asked. "And your money?"

"Sure, Mom." With nerves tense as coiled springs, Vicki felt too keyed-up to bristle at her mother's prosaic questions, and as they left the hush of their residential area, the rushing, whirring traffic demanded Mrs. Foster's undivided attention. Vicki tried to ease the stark realization that she was leaving home by memorizing fragments of the passing scene, shards of a city that yesterday had comprised her whole world. Pastel-tinted duplexes decorated the sun-swept hillsides, sailboats swooped and glided like graceful swans on the gray-green bay waters, and spread-winged gulls posed like white etchings against the azure sky. Could Hawaii's beauty match this?

They were late in reaching the airport. By the time Vicki confirmed her reservation, checked her luggage through, and dashed down the tubelike corridor to the flight gate, passengers were already boarding the silver jet. She gave her mother a darting kiss, a promise to write often, and a final wave. Then, like a mechanized doll forcing one foot ahead of the other, she joined her fellow travelers hurrying along the covered ramp toward the plane entrance. It was over. She had made the break, and neither she nor her mother had cried — visibly.

Too late for a choice spot beside a window, Vicki dropped into an aisle seat next to an elderly gentleman. After relaxing a moment, she stood up to stow her cosmetic case on the luggage rack. A stewardess promptly removed the bag, sliding it under Vicki's seat.

"No heavy items overhead, please," she said.

Vicki fastened her seat belt, then scanned safety information on printed cards in the pocket flap of the chair ahead of her. As the jet taxied slowly down the concrete runway, the stewardess recited last-minute instructions about emergency exits and oxygen masks before demonstrating the proper use of the life jackets.

Once airborne, Vicki relaxed and glanced at her watch. Two o'clock. The flight would take five hours, yet she knew that due to time changes, she would arrive in Honolulu around four P.M.

Vicki loosened her seat belt and leaned forward to peer out the window. The shimmering sun bewitched the ocean, changing it into a wash of molten silver. Then clouds blotted the scene. In seconds, a wispy mist fanned into an opaque veil, and the plane glided above a wonderland of snowdrifts and floating icebergs.

Vicki was in no mood for conversation with strangers. She felt drained and exhausted. Breaking from her family, parting from Greg, the decisions, decisions, decisions that had ended in pale compromise — all had taken vitality from her.

The stewardess served soft drinks. Vicki sipped her Coke, then closed her eyes and half dozed and half listened through earphones to hi-fi recordings of the New York Philharmonic. Although hours passed, it seemed only minutes before the stewardess appeared, distributing steaming-hot damp washcloths. Vicki wiped her face and hands, returned the cloth, and tightened her seat belt for landing, although she could see nothing but a slate-gray rolling ocean beneath them.

The plane dropped. Minutes later, the touchdown was smooth, and as soon as the pilot taxied to a stop, everyone gathered up his possessions.

After walking from the exit ramp to the ground, Vicki felt like a stranger in a foreign land. A feather of warm, damp breeze brushed her cheeks and fluffed her hair, and the smell of diesel exhaust blighted the air. She eased through the jostling crowd at the baggage-claim area and had no trouble spotting her bag; but as she picked it up, a brown hand lifted it from her and a boy reached up and placed a lei of lavender vanda orchids around her neck, then planted a kiss on her cheek.

"Aloha!" A dark-skinned boy with twinkling black eyes greeted her. "Welcome to Oahu, the aloha island."

"Aloha yourself!" Vicki looked into his smiling face and felt her fears and regrets slip away. "You must be Mark."

"Wrong, but take a second guess," her cousin said.

"Buzz!" Vicki glanced from Buzz to the taller boy who held her bag. "Then you're

Mark." She laughed. "I guess I didn't expect to find you all grown-up. Thank you both for the lei. I feel like a queen, and I'll wear it forever."

"You needn't be a queen to wear a lei." Mark's voice stung like a slap. "Anyway, it'll be wilted by tomorrow."

"I won't let it," Vicki said, again uneasy. "Back in the States I keep flowers for days in the refrigerator." She glanced up at her older cousin, but he was already heading from the terminal building and carrying her leaden suitcase as if it were no heavier than a handbag.

Buzz took her cosmetic case and walked at an unhurried pace as they followed his brother. "Don't mind Mark, Vicki. He's moody sometimes, but he doesn't mean to be impolite."

Clearly, Buzz wanted to explain Mark to her. The older boy led the way to an air-conditioned Buick, shoved the suitcase onto the back floor, and motioned Vicki to sit in the middle of the front seat. As she crawled in, she sniffed a spicy fragrance, then noticed a white carnation lei draped over the turn signal. Vicki wanted to ask whose it was, but Mark's cold, closed expression discouraged questions.

Mark gunned the motor, and both Vicki

29

and Buzz braced themselves against the dashboard as they slammed over a terrific bump.

"What was that?" Vicki asked.

"A silent policeman." Buzz grinned. "They're specially built humps in the pavement designed to stop drivers from speeding in front of the air terminal." He frowned at Mark, but his brother ignored him.

As they drove through surging traffic, Buzz chattered like a tour guide, pointing out spots of interest on either side.

"We're going to stop at Pier Nine, but we won't have time to look around today, Vicki. Mark has an errand to do before the *Canberra* sails, and we're due home for five o'clock dinner."

Mark was already turning into the parking lot, and finding an empty slot, he braked the Buick, grabbed the carnation lei, and skinned between parked cars toward an escalator that rotated like an endless black belt as it carried passengers to a ramp leading to the gangplank of the docked vessel.

"Mark's delivering that lei from Lili, one of our hotel guests, to her friend who sails tomorrow."

"Didn't your guest want to deliver the lei personally?" Vicki asked.

Buzz scowled. "She probably did. But

she's been upset about something lately. Anyway, she asked Mark to do it for her."

Vicki gave Buzz an appraising glance. If he were six inches taller, people might think that he and Mark were twins. They had both inherited curly black hair, obsidian eyes, and wide, mobile mouths. But there the resemblance ended. Buzz's eyes had a mischievous sparkle that matched his crescent-moon grin. Mark was different. Bitterness — or was it sadness? — shadowed her older cousin's face, and Vicki had yet to see him smile. But perhaps that was her fault.

"Buzz," she said, "have I done something to offend Mark? He seems sort of — of . . ."

Buzz sighed. "I know what you mean. But don't blame yourself. Of course, Mark resented your 'back-in-the-States' comment, because Hawaii's been in the union since nineteen fifty-nine, you know. Mark's naturally quiet, Vicki, and writing the Great American Novel makes him more moody than usual. Mom and I make allowances."

"I'll apologize to him for my blunder," Vicki said. "But, Buzz! I didn't know Mark was a writer. How interesting!"

"In college, Mark majored in business so he could help Mom run the hotel, but he spends every free minute either scribbling on the back of discarded envelopes or banging the typewriter keys. Paul Boint, I call him." Buzz grinned, then at Vicki's questioning glance, he answered. "It's sort of a scrambled pen name. Don't use it unless you're sure you can run faster than he can."

Mentally Vicki reversed the initial letters of the pen name, and while she smiled at Buzz's humor, she sensed that getting along with Mark was going to be harder than she had expected. How she wished she were going to be working with Sue instead! Yet this taciturn boy intrigued her. She could hardly wait to ask him about his writing.

The hands of the tower clock pointed to four-thirty when Mark returned to the car. Vicki tried to phrase an apology for her "back-in-the-States" blunder, but before she could rally her thoughts, Buzz resumed his endless chatter, identifying parks and ferns and trees and blossoms. As they passed a processing plant, the heavy, cloying odor of pineapple filled the car, but her cousins seemed to take such perfume for granted. Buzz recited names of the resort hotels they passed until Mark turned off the main street, drove several blocks into the sloping hills, and stopped in front of the Foster home.

A row of gaily painted coconuts separated

the asphalt driveway from the lush lawn. Surely Buzz must be responsible for the gay decoration.

"Last stop," Buzz said. "All out."

Vicki slid from the car and rested her hand on the shagged, pitted bark of a palm tree. "Hawaiian Reef Royal." She read the words from a sign supported by two carved images that guarded either side of the hotel entrance and which Vicki guessed to be likenesses of ancient Polynesian gods. Behind the ferocious-appearing figures with their monstrous mouths and staring eyes towered a sprawling two-story house. Vicki was speechless.

"Nothing fancy, but we like it." Buzz winked at her, but before she could ask him about the hotel's romantic-sounding name, he grabbed her cosmetic case and bounded away, leaving her alone with Mark.

"What a fabulous home." Vicki stepped back and almost stumbled over a hulking philodendron that entwined the trunk of a slim Norfolk pine. "No one told me you had a showplace lawn and a pineapple tree right in your front yard."

"*Pineapple* tree?" Mark shook his head. "Where?"

Vicki pointed. "There. The gray one with the feather-duster leaves and the tent-shaped roots growing above ground."

Mark snorted. "That's a pandanus tree. Tourist pineapple. That fruit tastes like wet wool sweaters; we never eat them."

"Well, I'm still impressed." Vicki turned around slowly, trying to see everything in sight.

"Don't let first impressions dazzle you." Mark frowned at her, and for a moment he reminded her of her father when he was about to deliver an unwanted lecture. "Mom and Buzz think Reef Royal's one short step from paradise, but I can tell you that it's common as coconuts when you're in working uniform on the business side of that lobby desk."

Mark's words bit like stinging splashes of sea water, and Vicki blinked as if to clear her vision. She pitied anyone who was immune to such captivating beauty. Following her cousin up two lava-rock steps onto a flagged patio that merged into an open sitting room decorated with potted orchids and caned rocking chairs, Vicki paused to absorb the scene.

"Lose something?" Buzz asked.

"I think I missed the front door." Vicki laughed.

"We have little use for doors." Buzz beamed with pride. "The temperature stays about the same the year around, and it seldom rains in this beach area. Most people like to be outside as much as possible, so this *lanai*, or open porch, is a popular place. There's another one at the back of the hotel, which faces toward the mountains. Most of the guests are out there now."

"Where's Aunt Noel?" Vicki asked.

"She's busy right now," Buzz answered. "We have orders to show you to Sue's room and let you rest until dinner."

Mark carried her blue bag down a hallway to the right of the lobby, waited until Buzz opened the louvered door, then thumped the bag on the floor inside the darkened room. "Someone'll call you for dinner," he said curtly.

The lobby telephone rang, and both boys hurried away, leaving Vicki feeling very much alone in her new home. Although the afternoon was warm, she shivered. Aunt Noel was too busy to greet her, Mark was obviously displeased with her presence, and now even good-natured Buzz had deserted her. Perhaps this exchange vacation had been a mistake. Maybe she should have stayed in San Francisco.

Buzz's lei and warm greeting had made her feel like someone very special, but Mark had a way of evoking all her feelings of self-doubt — those feelings that she had been accustomed to hiding behind her impulsive actions. Clearly, she was going to have to think of some way to win Mark's approval if she intended to enjoy her island vacation. She could only hope that he would be easier to please than her parents.

Chapter Three

Vicki waited for her eyes to adjust to the dim light before she approached a billowing hibiscus-print drapery that masked one side of Sue's room. Tugging the bulky fabric aside, she thought for a moment that it was the only barrier separating the bedroom from a small patio, or *lanai,* but closer inspection revealed a screen and a sliding glass door.

With both door and drapery open, Vicki stepped onto the *lanai* and inhaled a tropical potpourri of sea air and plumeria blossoms. A gnarled banyan tree dominated the parklike rear lawn of the Reef Royal, and two pink-blossomed plumerias shaded either corner of the building. While Vicki watched, a gray dove winged from an orchid bed to the lot behind the hotel where a tangled thicket encroached on Foster property despite the hibiscus hedge and file of royal palms rimming the grounds. Vicki's eyes were like darting humming birds hovering over the anthurium beds, the Golden Shower blossoms, the cereus vines. There was no compromising here. She loved everything she saw.

Reluctantly stepping back inside, Vicki was admiring the forest-green carpeting and the flame-orange bedspread that matched cushions on the bamboo bedroom chair when someone rapped on the door.

"Welcome to Reef Royal, Vicki!"

Vicki opened the door and smiled at the disarming, dark-haired beauty standing before her. "Aunt Noel! Oh, I'm so glad to be here! And Sue's room is a dream."

"Thank you, Vicki." Aunt Noel stepped into the bedroom. "We've tried to keep the family living quarters unchanged in spite of the rambling additions we've tacked onto the house. But you'll see all that later. Tell me about your parents. And Verne."

Again things seemed right. Vicki relaxed. It was just Mark's curdled mood that had alarmed her. Vicki bubbled family news as she breathed in a whispery jasmine odor and admired Aunt Noel's golden slippers and side-split, ankle-length sheath. While exotic, the outfit was in perfect harmony with her aunt's upswept hairdo, and Vicki thought this captivating relative must surely resemble her namesake, the Polynesian Princess Noelani of some forgotten age.

"I hate to rush you, Vicki." Aunt Noel

edged toward the doorway as Vicki finished speaking. "But the family always dines in my room at five o'clock. This early dinner hour allows a relaxed time together before the evening hotel duties begin. Why don't you freshen up in the bathroom across the hall, then come two doors to your left? We'll wait for you."

"Be right there, Aunt Noel." Vicki closed her door, slipped off her wilted jacket, and tucked in her shirt tail before stepping across the hall to wash. As water gushed into the aqua-blue basin, she touched the velvet nap of three peach-colored hibiscus sprinkled casually against a fan-shaped background of jungle-green palm fronds. Such beauty! Vicki wished that her parents and Greg were here to enjoy it with her.

Like a well-mannered escort, Buzz held Vicki's chair for her as the family gathered around a polished mahogany table in Aunt Noel's sitting room. Vicki noticed that their plates were on a tea cart, and as her aunt served them, Vicki smelled the savory aroma of fried fish and tartar sauce.

"Mahimahim *again*," Mark complained.

"The staple of the islands," Buzz said. "Ever tasted it before, Vicki?"

"I don't believe so." Vicki sampled a bite of the fish. "Why, it's delicious!"

"It's a relative of the golden dolphin," Aunt Noel explained. "We do serve it frequently. Last summer Mark caught a twenty-five pounder off the Kona coast."

"Is that near here?" Vicki asked.

Mark smiled slightly. "No, it's on the orchid island — the big isle of Hawaii."

"I'll never get all these islands straight in my mind," Vicki said. "Are there seven or eight?"

"Eight," Buzz said. "Niihau is called the forbidden island because it's privately owned and off limits for outsiders, and Kahoolawe is known as the Island of Death because it's a military target area and . . ."

"Enough!" Aunt Noel laughed.

"Such tongue-twister names." Vicki shook her head, and to her surprise Mark spoke.

"The Hawaiian language uses only twelve letters, Vicki, the five vowels plus H, K, L, M, N, P, and W. The vowel sounds are pronounced Ah, Ay, Ee, O, and Oo, and each vowel is enunciated separately. It's simple."

"I saw this word on a roadsign yesterday, Vicki," Buzz said. "It's a great one to practice. *Pi — pe — li — ne.*" Buzz spelled the word by syllables. "Try it."

Vicki hesitated like a swimmer reluctant

to make a plunging high dive. "Well, 'pi' would be 'pē,' 'pe' would sound like 'pay,' 'li' would be 'lee,' and 'ne' would sound like 'nay.' Peepayleenay?" She looked at Buzz, who was choking with mirth.

"Very good," he said. "But we Hawaiians just call it pipeline."

Realizing that she had blundered into Buzz's trap, Vicki laughed with the others.

"You'll have to forgive Buzz," Aunt Noel said. "That's his pet language joke, and it crowns his day to find a newcomer who'll fall for it."

As Mark chuckled with them, his mood mellowed a bit, and they all enjoyed a few minutes of relaxing conversation.

"Do you boys always dress alike?" Vicki studied their identical white trousers, white short-sleeved shirts, and brown print cummerbunds.

"This flashy outfit is known as our working uniform," Buzz said. "Gives the tourists a shot of local color. The white tends to make us look clean, and the cummerbunds imitate the barklike tapa cloth used by the ancient Hawaiians. We always dress like this in the dining room."

"You wait on tables?" Vicki asked.

"Everyone helps at mealtimes," Aunt Noel said. "I serve as cashier-hostess, Mark and two girls wait on tables, and Buzz fills water glasses and removes the used dishes."

"What jobs will I do?" Vicki asked as Buzz glanced at his watch and excused himself from the table.

"None today," Aunt Noel said. "After dinner, you may rest in your room or stroll about the grounds until the dining room closes. I'll stop by later and suggest an outline of tomorrow's chores."

From afar, a moaning whistle keened like a foghorn, and Aunt Noel and Mark rose. "Please excuse us, Vicki," her aunt said. "Buzz signals the opening of the dining room by sounding the conch. We'll see you later this evening."

Vicki returned to her room and listened to the clattering of dishes and the murmuring hum of voices. Opening her suitcase, she hung clothes in Sue's closet until she noticed three floor-length sheaths pushed to the back of the clothes rod. At first, Vicki thought Sue must have forgotten them, then she realized that her cousin would have slight use for such dresses in San Francisco.

When her belongings were arranged, Vicki slipped into her robe, turned down the bedspread, and stretched out on the cool green sheets.

"I shouldn't have disturbed you." Aunt Noel apologized as she entered the room later that night.

Vicki yawned. "Drat! I intended to stay awake, Aunt Noel. I meant to explore the grounds, but I must have dozed."

Vicki flipped a light switch, and in the glow from the overhead fixture her aunt looked tired and worn. Vicki pushed the bedroom chair forward.

"You must be exhausted, Aunt Noel."

"Only a bit weary." Aunt Noel curled into the chair. "I'll relax here while I outline your duties for you."

"I want to do everything Sue did," Vicki said. "I came here to work, you know. What were her chores?"

"I'll begin by saying that we have twenty guests at Reef Royal." Aunt Noel kicked off a slipper. "In the mornings I'll expect you to deliver fresh linens and make beds in ten rooms, then help in the dining area during lunch hour. By one-thirty you should be free for the afternoon. After our early family meal, we all help in the dining room until it closes."

"That sounds easy, Aunt Noel. Working here'll be like going to a party."

Aunt Noel sighed. "I hope so. But the routine may grow monotonous. Of course, you'll have one day off each week. We'll talk about that later. Free time is scheduled at the convenience of all the waitresses. Let's rest a bit more, then I'll show you the linen closets, the kitchen, and the dining area. It'll take you a while to adjust to your new surroundings."

"What do Mark and Buzz do to help?" Vicki asked.

"Mark's our business manager and night man," Aunt Noel said. "He's at the lobby desk from eleven P.M. until seven A.M."

"When does he sleep?" Vicki wondered if lack of rest might explain Mark's grumpiness.

"Mark's writing a book," Aunt Noel said. "He types from eleven until two when hotel activity is slight, then he sleeps on a cot near the lobby until I relieve him at seven. After napping a few hours during the morning, he's free until dinner time. Of course, he handles all the book work at his own convenience."

"I had no idea that Mark was a writer," Vicki said.

"He's always been interested in writing." Aunt Noel yawned. "He earned his university degree in business administration, but all his elective courses concerned penpushing."

44

"He's young to have already finished college," Vicki said.

"Mark skipped a grade in grammar school, and by attending university summer sessions, he managed to be graduated in three years. I wanted him to go to the mainland for advanced study. College is so important these days. If I'd stayed in school until I earned my teaching degree, this family would be better off than it is. I hate to see Mark repeating my mistake."

"Your hotel is wonderful, Aunt Noel. Would you really rather be a teacher?"

Aunt Noel shrugged. "I'd rather be able to support my family in a way that would involve less effort on their part. The life at Reef Royal is not an easy one. Mark feels tied here, yet he won't consider leaving. Sometimes I sense that he's deeply unhappy, but I suppose all writers have their moods."

Vicki wondered. Mark unhappy? Could that account for his sullen behavior? He had seemed more congenial at the dinner table, but perhaps that was an act for his mother's benefit.

"What does Buzz do, Aunt Noel?"

"I call him our public relations man. Of course, Mark complains that Buzz operates like a comedian on a joke and a smile, but

Buzz loves Reef Royal. He'd drop school in a minute if I'd let him work here full time. Although he already does his share of the work, he's taking typing this summer so he can help Mark at the desk."

"Anyone can tell that Buzz really is proud of the hotel," Vicki said.

Aunt Noel eased her foot into her shoe. "We used to have an excellent Filipino gardener, but after Tim died, the old fellow quit. I've gradually trained Buzz for the yard work. Earlier this summer he labeled all our plants. After telling hundreds of guests the names of each blossom and berry, even Buzz's smile grew thin."

"I can understand that." Vicki grinned.

"Buzz even started a paying business on his own, Vicki. Photography is his hobby, and he's set up a lobby display of color slides that he's offering for sale. But enough about the family. Reef Royal awaits. Come along."

Vicki followed her aunt to the linen closets, through the kitchen and dining area where a short, red-haired waitress rushed about her chores, and back to the main lobby.

"That girl we saw is Holly Hastings," Aunt Noel said. "Her father's stationed at Pearl Harbor, so she's living here while he's on an overseas assignment. Her room's just off the main kitchen; you'll probably meet her tomorrow."

Vicki nodded. "What does *kapu* mean, Aunt Noel? I see it printed on the swinging door to the kitchen."

"Oh, that's Hawaiian for 'keep out' or 'taboo.'" Aunt Noel laughed. "The cook hates to have guests invade his realm, so he stenciled that warning sign. By the way, Sue left you three uniforms in her closet. She's almost as tall as you, Vicki. I think they'll fit."

Vicki couldn't believe it. "Uniforms! You mean those three lovely dresses are work outfits?"

"That's right. More atmosphere for the guests."

"I can hardly wait to try them on, Aunt Noel. But you're exhausted! Just tell me which rooms I do tomorrow morning and I'll leave you alone." Vicki waited, but her aunt hadn't heard. She gazed into the back yard, and her pinched face looked like a map of worry lines.

"I beg your pardon, Vicki. What did you say?"

"Oh, Aunt Noel! What a nuisance for you to have to explain all these details."

"That's not bothering me, Vicki." Aunt Noel sighed. "I suppose you may as well know the worst. Lili Lanuoka, our most important guest, is threatening to move to Hale Maile."

"Lili Lanuoka." Vicki felt the name melt like butter on her tongue as they walked toward the family corridor. "But why is one guest more important than another? And what or where is Hale Maile?"

Aunt Noel paused at Vicki's doorway. "Lili is a direct descendant of the *alii*, and she was a cherished friend of your Uncle Tim's. We all love her dearly and want the best for her, but her presence at Reef Royal is of utmost importance to us and to the success of our business. Hale Maile is a new hotel across the street from us."

Before her aunt could continue, the telephone rang. "But Lili is my problem, Vicki. You have a good sleep, and I'll see you tomorrow. Perhaps you'll meet Lili while delivering linens."

Vicki listened to her aunt's heels tap like tack hammers as she hurried to the phone. Vicki left her bedroom door open, hoping that Aunt Noel would return. But the family wing of the house remained silent.

Draping her orchid lei over a chair on the *lanai*, where it would be cool, Vicki prepared for bed. Although she fully intended to work every bit as hard as Sue had, Vicki felt a twinge of guilt at coming to so busy a place and expecting a vacation.

Between cool sheets she puzzled over troubling questions as she lay in the silky darkness of the warm Hawaiian evening. The breeze wafted the perfume of plumeria, and in the distance, swaying palm fronds whispered in the night. Problems seemed misplaced in this paradise, yet Vicki sensed that Noelani Foster struggled with a matched set of worries, concerns that made Vicki's own college-versus-marriage decision fade into the background.

Chapter Four

The following morning Vicki awakened just as dawn smudged shell-pink streaks on the rain clouds that threatened the mountains. A muggy breeze dampened the *lanai,* and a persistent gray dove perched on a bamboo chair and called "coo-ka-ka-coo" to a friend who answered in turn.

Slipping into one of Sue's flattering dresses, Vicki stepped out into the morning. To her surprise, she saw Buzz, dressed in red hibiscus-patterned trunks, tugging at a green coil of garden hose as he watered a coconut palm whose bent trunk arched into the breeze like the curving prow of a Viking ship. Vicki returned Buzz's wave, retrieved her wilted lei from the chair, then stepped back inside to make her bed before appearing for breakfast. The distant clatter of dishes announced that the hotel staff was already working.

As Vicki approached the dining area, she saw that her dress was identical to those worn by the other waitresses. Suddenly she felt at home, as if she really belonged here. Before she had time to examine the rest of the covered patio, the red-haired girl hurried toward her.

"I'm Holly Hastings, and you must be Vicki." Her words tumbled out like peanuts from a broken bag.

"Right," Vicki answered. "I noticed you last night when Aunt Noel showed me around the hotel."

"Hate to greet you with problems, Vicki, but the grocery boy was late delivering the papayas. Would you have time to prepare five of them for the buffet table before the breakfast bunch arrives?"

"Sure thing." Vicki followed Holly through the *kapu* swinging door into the kitchen and over to a gleaming sink. "Any special instructions?"

"Halve the fruit, remove the seeds, and place a baby vanda in the small end of each serving. Miniki should bring the orchids any minute now. Oh, yes! Be sure to drop a lemon wedge on each plate." Holly pointed to a dish cupboard, then dashed off on other errands.

In spite of Holly's hurry-scurry attitude, Vicki took her time as she washed the oblong papayas, sliced them down the center, and scooped dark, clinging seeds from the peach-

51

colored flesh. Vicki almost drooled; the juicy fruit sparked her appetite. She was searching for the orchids Holly had mentioned when a tiny Oriental girl with black shoe-button eyes and blunt-cut patent-leather hair scurried toward her carrying a shallow cardboard box filled with lavender blossoms.

"Your flowers, Missy," she said in a low voice. "Many apologies for my tardiness."

Before Vicki could answer, the girl had slipped away like a streak of quicksilver.

"One blossom in each papaya half, then float the leftovers in cold water," Holly called over her shoulder as she charged the buffet table with a tray of plates.

Following instructions, Vicki waited for Holly to join her.

"Thanks loads, Vicki. But come on! If we're speedy we can grab a bite from the kitchen and eat on the *lanai* before serving time."

While Holly heaped a plate with Portuguese sausage, fried eggs, and an assortment of pineapples, mangoes, and bananas, Vicki poured a tumbler of milk and chose some sugary, spiced toast.

"Humph!" Holly plunked her plate on an inviting bamboo table. "Portuguese sweet bread and one glass of milk! You'll starve before lunch time."

Savoring the appetizing flavor of the toast, Vicki let a swallow of iced milk glide down her throat before answering. "I eat a scant breakfast, but I make up for it at lunch and dinner." The conversation ran low when Holly devoted herself to her scrambled eggs, and Vicki decided that she liked this rather tense yet good-natured girl who ate as if food might suddenly be rationed.

"Holly, what's an *alii?*" Vicki asked.

Holly smiled. "Years ago an *alii* was an Hawaiian chief or person of noble birth — you know, royalty."

"Aunt Noel told me that Lili Lanuoka is a descendant of the *alii,*" Vicki said. "Does she come around for breakfast? I'm dying to meet her."

Holly darted Vicki a questioning glance. "Not usually. She's a light eater, although you'd never guess that by looking at her."

"She's fat?" Vicki asked.

"Oh, no!" Holly grinned. "Most of the ancient Hawaiians were strapping people. According to what I've read, they were big-boned and they gorged like gluttons in order to maintain a whopping weight. Size was their status symbol."

"Lili Lanuoka is like this?" Vicki asked.

"No, no," Holly said. "She is large — she can't control her bone structure — but I'd guess you'd say she has a regal figure. I deliver a glass of guava juice to her room early every morning. That's her breakfast. So you're a writer, hmm?"

"Why, er, no." Holly's quick change of topic caught Vicki off guard. "What gives you that idea?"

"Oh, most newcomers who're interested in Lili are would-be authors." Holly tossed Vicki another probing glance. "You'll meet Lili soon enough. If you're doing Sue's duties, you'll find that Lili's room is first in your group. Pretty lucky, I call that!"

Did Holly always talk in riddles? There was no time to find out. An elderly gentleman strolled into the dining area, and Holly was up and away to her morning's work.

Vicki carried her own plate to the dishwasher, then, sauntering toward the linen closet, she determined not to let Holly's double-time cadence rub off on her. Vicki was eager to know just how much time her duties would occupy, and she was curious about Lili Lanuoka, but she was also eager to enjoy every moment of her stay in the islands. No hurry-flurry for her!

Vicki picked up the ring of keys hanging inside the linen closet door, arranged pink pastel sheets, pillow cases, and towels over her left arm, then approached apartment number one. Knocking lightly, she paused to listen. No answer. Vicki turned a key in the lock and stepped into the room.

She had expected a royal Hawaiian lady to live in an atmosphere of costly carpets, draperies, and brocades. This room was a surprise. Woven fiber mats covered the floor, shagged brown and white tapa cloth decorated the walls, and unpolished bamboo furniture gave the apartment a relaxed, rustic atmosphere. Staring, Vicki moved like an actress in a slow-motion film. She stalled at each chore, hoping that Lili Lanuoka might come in and allow her to discover for herself just why the respected lady was so important to Reef Royal.

But Lili didn't appear. Vicki finally left the apartment, her curiosity still at its peak. It was past midmorning when she finished the last of her assigned rooms and strolled back to her own quarters. She wrote Greg a long letter, then jotted notes to her mother and to Sue.

Although she still had a free hour before luncheon duty, she couldn't wait. Walking through the lobby, she paused to chat with her aunt, then headed on to the dining *lanai*. Holly waved from behind a mound of waxy-red anthurium blossoms and crystal bud vases that she was arranging for table centerpieces. Buzz called aloha from a swaying stepladder perch where he was replacing a burnt-out light bulb, but Mark ignored her. The whole area hummed with activity, and Vicki busied herself by folding napkins, arranging pandanus place mats, laying the silverware.

In the kitchen an excited dark-skinned man wearing a chef's cap babbled in a mixture of languages. Although Vicki missed his message, his working staff apparently understood him; anyway, under his direction the buffet table shaped into a thing of beauty.

Carrying a basket of crimson and gold hibiscus blossoms, Mark approached Vicki. "Drop these on the table. You have five minutes before the dining room opens."

Vicki noticed that Mark's vocabulary seemed to lack the words *please* and *thank you,* but she was too astonished at his request to be miffed. "But where shall I place the basket, Mark? There's no space."

"Not the whole basket," Mark scowled. "Just scatter the blossoms at random. You can't go wrong."

Vicki followed orders, finding that Mark was right. Plumped down casually between the appetizing dishes, the brilliant blossoms added a dazzling touch to the luncheon table.

Once the diners had filled their plates and seated themselves, Vicki helped pour coffee and tried to see that the guests had everything they needed for an enjoyable lunch. She had been so busy with her duties that until they began strumming ukuleles, she failed to notice the three Hawaiian ladies now posed like noble Polynesian statues in front of a green Japanese silk screen.

Vicki stood open-mouthed. All three women were tall, but she guessed that the one in the center must stand over six feet in height.

"So now you've seen Lili," Holly said as she dashed to the kitchen to replenish a platter of baked ham and cheese.

"Which one?" Vicki called after her.

"The tallest one. The one in the middle."

"But is she working here?" Vicki asked. "I thought she was a prized guest." Turning to look at Holly, Vicki found that the girl had hurried off.

Vicki joined the guests in applauding the trio as they finished a medley of lilting Hawaiian songs. But once the music stopped, the diners drifted from the *lanai* until the area was deserted except for employees.

Vicki saw Mark eating alone, and she filled a plate for herself and joined him. She would rather have had lunch with Holly or

57

with Buzz, but she remembered an overdue apology, and she wanted to right things between herself and her cousin. Sipping her iced tea, which was garnished with a fresh pineapple spear, she gave Mark her full attention.

"I'm sorry about that thoughtless 'back-in-the-States' comment I blurted out yesterday afternoon, Mark. How about another chance? Buzz informed me that the proper expression is 'on the mainland.' I'll remember that."

"It's not all that important." Mark grinned for an instant, then his face clouded. "I suppose I'm the one who should offer apologies. I don't intend to be such a sourball, Vicki. It's just that sometimes I get fed up. Have you ever felt — trapped? Here I am, tied down here like — like an *adult*. When I think of Sue having a ball on the mainland, and when I see you here play-acting as a hotel employee, it's almost more than I can stand."

Mark's words stunned Vicki. She felt hurt, angry, helpless. "I'm hardly play-acting, Mark, and Sue's working an eight-hour day in San Francisco. If you hate it here, why not cut out? Your mother said she wished you'd study on the mainland."

"As if it were that simple," Mark snapped.

"I may be a grouch, but I'm no heel. Mother needs a man here; it's my duty to stick around. But I do hate it. And with Sue attending a mainland college in the fall, the situation will be even worse. We'll have to hire a replacement, and no outsider is ever as dependable as a member of the family."

"What would you do if you had a free choice?" Vicki asked.

A dreamy expression glazed Mark's eyes, and he spoke almost as if he were talking to himself. "I'd find a pleasant, deserted island somewhere, and I'd think and write and loaf and read and then think some more."

"Spoken like a true beach bum." Vicki laughed, but for a moment she thought she understood Mark a bit better. Hadn't she delighted in leaving her problems in San Francisco and coming to the islands?

"I didn't say I'd spend my whole life lazing in the sun — just enough of it to discover what I really think about things. I might wind up believing that managing a hotel is one way of making a worthwhile contribution to society. But I resent being pushed into the decision like clay into a mold. I need time to decide issues for myself."

"Can't you think right here?" Vicki asked. "Sort of as you go along?"

"Not clearly," Mark answered. "I keep getting the urgent mixed up with the important, until I'm not really sure of anything."

"You seem to be sure that your duty is to stay at Reef Royal," Vicki pointed out.

"You disagree?" Mark's tone challenged.

"I honestly don't know, Mark," Vicki said. "But a brilliant writer, Robert Louis Stevenson, once said that people underrate their duty to be happy. Perhaps Aunt Noel would rather see smiles than scowls."

"Around Mom my humor is okay, and she does see me smile." Mark frowned. "I'm not so stupid as to let her know how I feel. It's not her fault that she's a widow. But I wouldn't expect you to understand. I'll bet ten to one that you have a boyfriend waiting on the mainland. You'll probably be married before you're nineteen, and begin the great rat race to keep two cars in the garage that is attached to a house that is just a trifle larger than your neighbor's."

Vicki felt as if Mark were looking through her, as if she were a glass statue. She wondered if he suspected what compromises she had made with herself and her parents.

"You have a personal dislike for houses and cars?" Vicki asked.

"Wish I did," Mark said. "The truth is, I like material possessions as well as anyone.

But at the moment they are neither urgent nor important. Right now all I want is some time to myself."

"What can I say, Mark?" Vicki asked. "I certainly don't have the answer you need."

"At least you admit it."

Vicki couldn't find words to reply. Mark was an enigma. She could have sympathized with him had he said he hated his job. But he hadn't said that at all. In fact, he had hinted that he might even devote his life to the hotel business. Vicki suddenly suspected that Mark was afraid — afraid to accept adult responsibility.

"Don't look at me that way, Vicki," Mark said. "Let's forget this whole conversation. I was being unfair. Cancel everything I've said, and let's be friends, okay?"

"That's what I wanted all along." Vicki squeezed out a smile and hoped it was convincing. She couldn't decide whether to feel angry at Mark or sorry for him, but she knew they would be seeing a lot of each other this summer. That was reason enough to try to get along. Perhaps their mutual interest in writing would draw them into friendship. Maybe when she and Mark were better acquainted, they would exchange tips on writing. But right now she had no intention of revealing her secret ambition.

"Tell me about Lili Lanuoka, Mark." Vicki tossed out a new topic. "Why is so grand a lady entertaining here in the dining area, and why is she so important to Reef Royal and the Fosters?"

"Lili's a great old girl, Vicki. Once you meet her, you'll never be the same again." Mark's whole mood mellowed as he spoke of Lili. "She's important to us because she's our friend. Lili inherited fabulous wealth from her ancestors, but she also earned a fortune in her own right. She was educated by the granddaughter of one of the first missionary families that came to these islands. She writes, you know."

"What sort of writing does she do?" Vicki asked.

"Lili wrote the words to the hit song 'Lanoloma Star.' "

"Really!" Vicki hummed the poignant melody.

"After retiring from the service, Dad practiced law, and he saw to it that Lili received the proper royalties for her work. Like most Hawaiians, Lili loves to sing. As a favor to us, she offered to entertain here in the hope of drawing customers to Reef Royal. Although she's a big name in Hawaii, she accepts no money for her services. Lili has no relatives except an old aunt over on

Maui, but even so, Mother had a hard time persuading her to live here with us as one of our family."

"How generous." Vicki buttered a roll and watched Mark poke at a lettuce salad.

"Mother tried to be generous," Mark said, "but, as usual, we seemed to end up deeper and deeper in debt to Lili."

"How can that be?" Vicki asked. "She entertains in exchange for a home with people who love and care for her. Seems more than fair to me."

"You probably haven't noticed, Vicki, but this location isn't exactly the greatest. Most tourists want a spot right on the beach, and while we sit high enough to see the ocean from the front *lanai,* we're not within easy walking distance. When we first opened, we lost money in spite of Lili's entertaining. But her mind's an idea factory. Her singing's amateurish, but she has a talent for creative writing — still composes a weekly column for the *Aloha Gazette,* a newssheet slanted to the tourist trade."

"How does that concern Reef Royal?" Vicki asked.

"Lili established an annual writing contest and offered a year's university scholarship as first prize. Also, she publishes an anthology of the best ten stories entered in the competition. Besides all this, Lili agreed to advise and help all would-be writers in residence — either guests or employees."

Vicki drained her tea glass and tried to hide her excitement. "Did you attend college on her scholarship?"

"No," Mark said. "I majored in business. But once we advertised Lili's contest and services, we had more guests than we could handle, and we're really never short of employees as are some hotels. Writers enjoy this relaxing atmosphere, and Lili keeps busy reading and criticizing manuscripts. So far, we've built two new wings onto the hotel."

"Now I understand why Lili's leaving has upset you. But surely Aunt Noel can talk her out of it. Has someone offended Lili?"

"That's the puzzling part of the affair," Mark said. "We have no idea why she's leaving. All we know is that she's moving across the street to Lafe Yankton's Hale Maile before the next full moon."

"A charming way of stating an unwelcome fact," Vicki said.

"Lili's expression, not mine," Mark replied. "Sometimes she comes on very Hawaiian, but no matter how you say it, she's moving out in ten days."

"That's too bad." Vicki knew her words

were inadequate, but although she could think of nothing better to say, she realized that Reef Royal faced a serious loss. A writer in residence! And a scholarship contest! In spite of her determination to keep her writing ambitions a secret, these thoughts excited her and added a new dimension to her vacation setting. Was she eligible for Lili's contest? Would Lili help her get started in writing? Before she could ask Mark, he scowled, scraped his chair back, and without excusing himself, picked up his barely touched lunch and left Vicki sitting alone.

Chapter Five

Vicki was through eating, and although she resented Mark's deserting her at the table, she decided to follow Buzz's example and make allowances. As Reef Royal's unwilling business manager, Mark did have a lot of things to consider, and Vicki realized that Lili Lanuoka's unaccountable decision to move affected her, too. If Reef Royal lost patrons, she might soon find herself headed back home minus both job and vacation. Back to San Francisco and the problems she thought she had ditched for the summer.

Vicki suddenly thought about her parents and wondered if they were lonesome with both Verne and herself away for the summer. But how silly! Parents didn't get lonesome. Or did they? Vicki really hadn't had time to be homesick yet, but when she thought about her mother and father she felt a strangling ache deep in her throat. Was it possible to love someone and at the same time to resent them? Right now — right this minute — she would love to see her mother.

But Vicki faced the truth. She knew that if her mother were here, or if she herself were in San Francisco, they'd probably visit not over ten minutes before the painful argument would start again. Her mother would lecture on the joys of college and the perils of marriage until Vicki would feel impelled to defend her own viewpoint. It was better that they were separated; the arguments got them nowhere. In spite of an avalanche of words there was still a basic lack of communication.

Vicki carried her plate to the dishwasher as she planned her leisure hours. A free afternoon to do as she pleased! But what to choose? Her morning's activities left her with barely enough energy to drag to her room and flop across the bed like a limp rag doll.

I'll rest for thirty minutes, then I'll catch a bus to the beach, Vicki decided as she kicked off her straw sandals. But the next time she opened her eyes it was almost four o'clock, and her aunt was calling to her.

Vicki popped up and smoothed her hair. "Come in, Aunt Noel."

"Open the door, please."

Vicki padded barefoot over the velvet-soft carpet to admit her aunt who was holding a polished koa-wood tray covered with an orange linen napkin. A breath of air fanned through the opened door, and Vicki whiffed the pungent fragrance of freshly brewed coffee.

"I forgot to mention that Sue usually took Lili an afternoon snack." Aunt Noel rested the hand-carved tray on the dressing table. "Of course, I can deliver it, but I thought you might like to meet Lili. She'll expect you to have coffee with her."

"Oh, Aunt Noel! I'd love to take the tray! I'll even choke down a cup of coffee if necessary."

Aunt Noel smiled. "Sue dislikes ordinary coffee too, Vicki, but this brew is different. Perhaps you'll like it. Lili has a friend who owns a coffee plantation near the Kona coast and who sends her freshly ground berries."

"I'm so excited about talking to Hawaiian royalty that I could drink hemlock without noticing the flavor," Vicki said. "Was Lili's father really a king?"

"No." Aunt Noel shook her head. "The monarchy ended with Hawaii's annexation to the United States in 1898 — a sad day for many Hawaiians. But through her mother's side of the family Lili is a direct descendant of King Kamehameha the Great. Now scoot with that tray before the coffee cools."

Wondering a bit about her aunt's words concerning annexation day, Vicki slipped into *holomuu* and sandals and carried the snack to Lili's apartment. At her first tap the door opened, and as Lili motioned her inside, Vicki smiled up at the towering, silver-haired woman.

"You must be Vicki." Lili's lilting voice rippled, and she ducked her head to keep from hitting the ceiling chandelier. "I noticed you today at lunch time. You look enough like Tim Foster to be his daughter. Here, I'll take the tray."

"Uncle Tim was my father's twin, Mrs. Lanuoka."

"Please call me Lili, Vicki."

Vicki was suddenly tongue-tied. "Lili," she repeated as she watched her hostess bend double in order to place the refreshments on an unusual, low table. Lili's expressive brown eyes fascinated Vicki. One moment they danced in child-like wonder, and the next moment they seemed to belong to a person older than the very islands.

"Have a cup of coffee, and I'll tell you about my room if you're interested," Lili said.

Lili's cordial words helped Vicki relax, and her voice returned.

"Oh, please do. I don't mean to stare or to

be nosey, but I noticed your furnishings this morning when I delivered the linens. This coffee table! I've never seen anything like it." Vicki ran her fingers lightly over the unplaned surface of the shallow dish-shaped table top which was supported by two crudely-carved figures, a man and a woman.

Lili smiled. "The table belonged to my great-grandmother who used it as a serving dish at royal *luaus* or feasts. It was designed to hold and serve a whole pig which was first wrapped in green ti leaves, covered with red-hot stones, and roasted for hours in a deep pit in the ground."

"It makes a unique table, Lili. My, but this coffee *is* good." Vicki spoke the truth. The coffee had a tantalizing mellowness that she really enjoyed. "Isn't this brand ever shipped to the st . . . er . . . the mainland?" Vicki felt herself blush as she almost repeated her error.

"Oh, it is. It is," Lili said. "But on the mainland it is blended with South American coffee. Only here in the islands do we enjoy the undiluted Kona flavor."

"I'll bet there's a story about this floor covering, too." Vicki added another sugar cube to her coffee. "I noticed that all the other apartments are carpeted, yet this matting seems in perfect taste."

"These woven fibers are identical to those used in the old Hawaiian grass shacks." Lili lifted the edge of the thatch-tan covering and revealed another mat underneath. "They're woven from leaves of the pandanus tree, and when a mat wears thin I simply place a new one on top. I've taught Buzz and some of his friends to do the weaving." Lili walked across the room and touched the rough wall covering. "My great-grandmother hammered the tapa cloth which you see here, and the coarse net that I've adapted as a table cover was once used for fishing on my grandfather's outrigger canoe. I dislike museums and useless artifacts, so I've converted these few symbols of bygone Hawaii into functional bits of household equipment. They help to remind me of who I am."

Vicki wondered what Lili meant by her last remark. Did one need to be reminded that one was royalty? "Mark tells me that you're a professional writer and that you also encourage others to try." Vicki changed the subject, although her eyes still strayed to the fascinating ornaments from a pagan culture.

Lili nodded. "Do you write?"

"Oh, no." Vicki felt like a child half-wanting to get by with a fib, yet half-hoping to be caught and punished.

"Your face tells the truth," Lili said. "Either you write or you want to write. Which is it?"

"I do keep a journal," Vicki admitted, "but I've never written so much as an article or a short story — just impressions and ideas. I understand Mark's the author in our family."

Lili ignored the subject of Mark. "Your journal, Vicki. Perhaps you'd show it to me sometime."

Vicki felt her face flush steaming hot. She hated to risk offending Lili, but she had no intention of showing her scribblings to anyone — not even to Hawaiian royalty.

"I'm afraid . . ." Her voice trailed off.

"I won't pry." Lili's eyes gleamed like black pearls. "But if you change your mind about writing you might consider entering my scholarship contest. I understand you're ready to go to college this coming fall."

"I've finished high school," Vicki said, "but I plan to take a business course for a few months, be married, and then work to help my husband through law school."

"Are you not young for marriage?" Lili's eyes clouded, and she reminded Vicky so much of a wise old owl that she felt uneasy. She knew she had impulsively blurted out too much — revealed too many plans, but something about this friendly, understanding person seemed to draw the words from deep inside herself. She hadn't expect opposition.

"Mark told me about your writing scholarship and the annual anthology of stories." Vicki tried to draw Lili's interest back to her own life. "It's a wonderful thing for you to do."

"The granddaughter of a missionary family which came to the islands to help the natives taught me about creative writing," Lili said. "The missionaries and their descendants built the islands into what you see today, but many of those *haoles*, or white people, expected too little of us. Being naturally a carefree people, many Hawaiians contented themselves by drifting through life accomplishing nothing and depending on others to care for them. But my teacher was different. She instilled in me the ideas that every human is put on earth to perform some useful function and that a person can do anything that she is determined to do."

"And you proved her right." Vicki guessed.

"I've known some success," Lili said modestly. "It was never easy for me to give up the ways of thinking of my parents and accept the startling ideas of my teacher, but I applied my mind to her lessons, and I was able to set a goal for myself, to find a meaningful way of life."

"She must have been inspiring," Vicki said.

"Although the Fosters think I am only trying to help them, the scholarship is my way of saying thank you to a great teacher." Lili rose to her full height and strolled to the glass doors that separated her apartment from a private *lanai*. "If you are interested in submitting anything in this year's contest, you should get your manuscript to me before the deadline ten days from now. You won't have time to write anything of great length, but budding talent can reveal itself in a short story."

"I've only been here such a few days, Lili. Surely I wouldn't be eligible to try for such an important prize." Although Vicki's future plans excluded college, Lili's contest intrigued her, the goal of publication held great appeal.

Vicki visualized her by-line in a children's magazine, her name on the dust jacket of an award-winning juvenile novel. Writing here in this setting would offer a unique opportunity for her to test her talent. No one in San Francisco need know if she failed miserably. By submitting a contest entry she would, at least for her own satisfaction, poke holes in

Greg's accusation that she had a closed mind concerning her future. And what was it that Lili's teacher had said? Anyone can do anything that she is really determined to do?

Lili broke into Vicki's thoughts. "Anyone living at Reef Royal is eligible to enter my contest. I've been reading manuscripts ever since the contest closed last summer, and I've almost narrowed the field to the stories which will appear in this year's anthology, but any manuscripts I receive in the next ten days will get painstaking consideration. Think it over, Vicki. The world opens many doors to those who write."

"Speaking of doors, Lili, is it true that you're leaving Reef Royal and moving to Hale Maile?" Vicki was glad to change the subject.

"That is true." Lili's voice rang like a closing cadence, but Vicki blurted her most pressing question before she lost her nerve.

"Why? Why are you moving, Lili? Have the Fosters offended you?"

"I have reasons that you would never understand." Lili's voice died, and her smile vanished like water on dry sand. Vicki skipped to a safer topic.

"I enjoyed your singing in the dining room this noon, Lili. Who were the other trio members?"

"Naloma Wong and Leilani Hawagasa are childhood friends from the garden island of Kauai. We each married and moved to Oahu, but our paths parted for many years. Then, as we were widowed, we gradually drifted back together again. It's a pleasure for us to meet and sing and strum our guitars as we did in our girlhood." Lili's eyes were mirrors of the past, and Vicki felt that the magnificent old lady must often long for the land of her youth.

"Wong? Hawagasa?" Vicki questioned. "Those don't sound like Hawaiian names to me."

"The ladies are two of the few remaining pure-blooded Hawaiians in the islands," Lili said. "For many heart-breaking years they were ostracized by their families for marrying out of their race. Naloma chose a Chinese farmer who owned his own taro patch, and Leilani's Japanese husband was a grocer. The ladies were never wealthy, but they were happy and contented. Gradually their island families accepted them once more; those social barriers were lowered long ago. Mrs. Wong now supports herself by making and selling leis in a charming thatch shack near Waikiki beach, and Mrs. Hawagasa opens her home in the evenings to tourists searching for sukiaki dinners."

"I hope you'll introduce me to your friends tomorrow," Vicki said. "But now I must return the coffee tray and freshen up for dinner. I've enjoyed our visit ever so much."

"Then come again," Lili said. "And perhaps you'll think a bit about writing and about sharing your journal with me. I'd be pleased if you would."

Vicki closed the door behind herself and walked slowly back to her room. Setting the tray on the dressing table she paused to think. Mark was right. She'd never be the same again now that she'd met Lili Lanuoka. Vicki could pin-point no sudden change that was apt to be noticed by even her closest friends. But the regal lady's youthful dignity made Vicki feel that she had been exposed to an intriguing mixture of excellence drawn from both an ancient culture and a modern civilization.

In a few fleeting minutes Lili had managed to stretch Vicki's imagination until her thoughts wouldn't ease back into their once-comfortable channels. Someone had tip-toed through her private, secluded world opening windows that might never be firmly closed again. Her pat little plan for an accelerated business course, then a headlong rush into marriage lost some of its glamour. Perhaps she *could* write if she put her mind to it. Perhaps, as Lili said, she could do anything in the world if she only wanted to badly enough.

Well, she wanted to. Her sudden, deep desire to start writing immediately surprised her and at the same time left her with a feeling of inadequacy. She couldn't even remember the last time she'd really tested herself — really tried to achieve something difficult, something of importance. She might fail. Perhaps she really was as mediocre as her high-school grades attested.

How could she dream of writing anything worth reading when she couldn't even learn the answer to a simple question — an answer which might decide her own fate as well as the future of the Fosters' hotel? Why was Lili Lanuoka leaving her friends and an apartment that she obviously loved? In what way did she consider Hale Maile superior to Reef Royal?

Chapter Six

Vicki soon learned that dinner duty at Reef Royal was the most pleasant event in her working day. Feeling the liquid, gliding softness of the tropical evening dissolve all tensions, she watched the hotel guests dine in an atmosphere of old Hawaiian charm and grace. From the orange light flickering from patio torches she saw that most of the men were conservatively dressed, but the majority of the ladies looked like travel-poster models. Billowing Hawaiian muumuus, Japanese silk kimonos, and flowing Filipino gowns with butterfly sleeves sparked the dining area like gems from a scattered collection of crown jewels. In the background a hi-fi played island ballads while the spicy-sweet fragrance of plumeria and carnations drifted in the breeze like a silent aloha. Being so overwhelmed by beauty, Vicki could barely concentrate on her work.

The dinner hour sped by. And although it was only nine o'clock when she left the kitchen, Vicki was ready for bed; she felt as if she'd lived a week in the jet-propelled hours between dawn and dark.

On the following morning Vicki slept until well past sunrise, and it was lunch time before she saw either of her cousins. She watched Lili Lanuoka, Mrs. Wong, and Mrs. Hawagasa end their song-fest by inviting Buzz to join them. Buzz seemed shy at first, but he grinned and sang several verses of a humorous ballad concerning Princess Poopooly and her papayas while the statuesque Hawaiians accompanied him on their ukuleles and guitars.

"Neat number, Buzz," Vicki called as they finished chores in the dining room. "Didn't know you sang."

"All Hawaiians sing." Mark came up behind her, and Vicki heard the scowl in his voice. "It's more of a vice than a virtue."

"Jealousy, jealousy!" Buzz replied condescendingly. Draping a dishtowel around his slim waist he danced a comic hula as he sang about Lola O'Brien, the Irish Hawaiian. Vicki was so entertained by the song that she didn't notice Mark stalk away, but when Buzz finished his burlesque, they were alone.

"What's doing this afternoon, Vicki?"

"I'd like to go to the beach." Vicki followed Buzz to the hotel lobby. "I've heard these Hawaiian waters are warm winter and summer."

"Would you believe thirteen months of the year?" Buzz grinned.

"Spoken like the voice of the Honolulu Chamber of Commerce," Vicki teased. "How far to the beach?"

Buzz pretended to count on his fingers. "About nine blocks as the albatross flies, but a bit farther if you're a people and have to walk. Think I'll tag along with you if you don't mind. Meet me out front in four and a half minutes? It's only a block to the bus stop."

In her room Vicki sighed as she slipped into the canary-yellow bathing suit she'd bought especially for her vacation. She hadn't definitely decided to reveal her literary ambitions by entering Lili's contest, but she had planned to write this afternoon. Yet the lure of the beach was like a Lorelei song that distracted her. She tried to rationalize by telling herself she was gathering material, but she knew she was postponing settling down to work on a writing project. She was frightened at the thought of really trying something so important to her.

Pulling on a terry-cloth robe, Vicki hurried out to meet Buzz. He was waiting. Leaving the Reef Royal grounds, Vicki glanced toward Hale Maile, where a stumpy, fat man dressed in white paced across the grass. Vicki shuddered. Here among Hawaii's medley of flashing colors such a costume had all the allure of a pale fish belly.

"Who's that, Buzz?"

"Lafe Yankton." Buzz snipped the words, then as a mongoose scurried across the lawn, he gave her a rambling history of that weasel-like animal originally imported to help control the rat population. Buzz was still chattering like a Mynah bird when they reached the bus stop. Vicki groaned.

"What gives?" Buzz darted her a questioning look. "Forget something?"

Vicki eyed the rolling storm clouds overhead. "In case you hadn't noticed, we're getting wet." She sighed. "We'd better go back."

Buzz stretched one hand into the misting rain, touched his tongue gingerly to his fingers, and announced, "We're safe, Vicki. That's not rain; it's pineapple juice!"

Before he finished his explanation the mist had evaporated, and they waited under a pandanus tree until the bus arrived. Once at the beach, Vicki followed Buzz along a path leading between two hotels and down to a public swimming area. Shading her eyes with her hand she gazed out to sea where a meringue of whitecaps laced the undulating blue waves. Closer to the beach the shallows shaded to a shimmering green, and at the shore line the frothy surf heaved in, swirling and churning the sand to the color of a root-beer float. If she could only paint instead of merely sketch! What fun it would be to catch the ever-changing water on canvas.

"Race you in, Buzz." Slipping from her robe Vicki spread her fluffy towel on the dry sand, then noticed that Buzz was staring into the distance.

"Hey, Vicky! There's a catamaran loading with tourists down at the pier. If I hurry I can just make it. Be back in a jiff. You stay here."

"What's up?" Vicki asked. It surprised her that easy-going Buzz was capable of such a surge of excitement.

Before Buzz could answer, a smiling dark-skinned boy balancing a surfboard under one arm and carrying a soft drink cup in his bandaged right hand approached them.

"Hey, Penolo," Buzz called. "Meet my cousin, Vicki. Vicki, this is Penolo Pulianano — Penni for short. He'll see that you don't drown until I get back."

Buzz raced away, and Vicki felt herself flush with embarrassment as she faced this boy whom Buzz had railroaded into looking after her. As if she couldn't take care of herself!

"Penni," she said, "Buzz was only kidding. I don't need a chaperone. I'll be perfectly okay." Vicki knew she was blushing more furiously as the handsome Hawaiian looked her over, obviously pleased with what he saw.

"Buzz's wish is my command." Penni plopped his surfboard onto the sand, sat on it, and made room for Vicki beside him. "Where have the Fosters been hiding you?"

"I arrived only two days ago, and I've been working at Reef Royal." Vicki sifted sand through her fingers and felt the sun burn against her shoulders as she studied her exciting companion. His flashing white teeth accented his umber features, his red swim trunks matched the crimson hibiscus blossom tucked casually behind one ear, and against his muscled chest a hook-shaped chunk of ivory and a carved ebony figure dangled from a silver chain.

As he saw her eye them, Penni touched the trinkets with a yellow-stained forefinger, and before Vicki could ask the questions bursting to her lips, he supplied the answers.

"The white one's a whale's tooth, and the black one's an image of the ancient Hawaiian god, Lono. The whale's tooth once marked nobility, but now it's just a trinket readily available at the nearest souvenir stand."

Vicki laughed. This boy fascinated her. His low, purring voice was restful as velvet, yet something about his eyes put her on guard. Penni's impertinence dismayed Vicki, but at the same time, his undisguised admiration flattered her.

"Where did Buzz go in such a dash?" Vicki asked. "He mentioned a catamaran whatever that is."

"That's that red, twin-hulled sailing vessel." Penni stood up and pointed. "See, it's docked at the pier. Buzz goes there to dive for coins. He's earning money to pay for a surfboard that I sold him. Want to go watch?"

Vicki stood and brushed the sand from her suit. "You're a surfboard salesman?"

"I turn a deal now and then." Penni shrugged his shoulders. "But I'm hired by the Coral Towers Hotel to give surfing lessons to their guests. That's my real job."

"Perhaps you shouldn't leave the beach," Vicki said. "I'll walk ahead to the pier and wait for Buzz."

"Trying to ditch me?" Penni asked.

Again Vicki felt herself blush. "Of course

not, Penni. I just don't want you to lose your job because of me."

"Penolo Pulianano!" A voice boomed over a loudspeaker. "Penolo Pulianano! Report to lobby."

"See, they've missed you already," Vicki said.

"Worst luck!" Penni turned to go back to the hotel, then hesitated. "What are you doing tonight, Vicki? I'd like to show you the town. Will you let me meet you at Reef Royal after you get off work? Say around nine o'clock?"

Vicki's mind formed the word *no;* she was Greg's girl, yet she nodded in agreement as if she were a puppet and some unseen master were pulling the strings. Penni winked at her, turned, and sauntered back toward his hotel. As he disappeared into the crowd Vicki felt as if some magic spell had been broken. How could she have agreed to go out with this stranger! She didn't want Penni or anyone else to think she was a cheap pick-up. But after all Buzz had introduced them. She trudged through the shifting sand arguing with herself until she came to the pier.

At first she didn't see Buzz, then his dripping head broke surface to the left of the catamaran and he hoisted himself onto some pilings to rest. He had hardly caught his breath when a man in a kelly-green aloha shirt spun a quarter high into the air. The coin glinted in the sun then plunked into the water. Buzz jack-knifed into the waves and stayed under so long that Vicki began to worry. In the meantime the boat left the pier and the tourists turned their attention to their guide.

Vicki scanned the water where Buzz had disappeared, but to her surprise he surfaced on the other side of the pier and swam toward shore.

"How'd you do?" Vicki called as he panted in to meet her.

"Two thirty-five." Buzz grinned and patted the zippered pocket of his trunks. "And did I ever earn every cent! One guy was throwing nickels, for Pete's sake! Where's Penni? Did you test the surf?"

"Penni was called to work, and I'll have to swim another time. I'm not used to this sun; I can feel myself getting a real burn. You stay as long as you want, but I'm going home."

"I'll go with you," Buzz agreed. "Enough ocean for one day."

Even Buzz was silent on the bus ride back to Reef Royal, and Vicki was contented to keep her disturbing thoughts to herself. Penolo Pulianano — Penolo Pulianano.

Against her will the name sang through her mind like a pagan chant.

Once back in her room, Vicki stretched out on the bed for a few minutes before sitting down at the desk to write to Greg. To her surprise she stalled after the opening two words. Of course, she missed Greg. Of course, she wanted to share every moment of their separation with him. Yet the blank paper stared at her accusingly, and it took a forced effort and much time for her to fill both sides of the page. Somehow Greg seemed remote as a dream, and San Francisco a city in a fairy-tale book. Although she wished it otherwise, Penni Pulianano crowded into her thoughts, and it was his name that she mentioned first when the family gathered for dinner.

"Penni Pulianano!" Mark's fork clattered to his plate. "You're surely not going out with *that* beach bum. Where did you meet *him?*"

"Mark!" Aunt Noel frowned at her son. "Tell us; where did you meet Penolo, Vicki?"

"I introduced them," Buzz said. "Penni's an all-right guy."

"Just because you swallowed his hard-sell on that crummy surfboard you won't admit what a creep he is," Mark said. "And ten percent carrying charges!"

"The board has a custom built keel and a brand new paint job, Mark. It's worth every cent of the price," Buzz insisted.

"Aunt Noel," Vicki said. "I thought Penni seemed nice enough, but if you'd rather I didn't see him, I'll break the date. It's not really important."

"You needn't cancel your plans." Aunt Noel smiled. "Now, Mark." She shushed her son with a look. "You may not approve of Penni, but Vicki's old enough to choose her own friends. If Penni is as unworthy as you say, I'm sure Vicki will sense this and end their friendship."

Vicki hid her surprise. No arguments here. Aunt Noel wasn't going to lecture or argue — she trusted Vicki's judgment. Basking in this pleasing knowledge, Vicki smiled at Mark who wasn't even looking at her.

"Well, Mother, surely you're not going to let her go out with him *alone!*" Mark said.

"Would you like to chaperone?" Aunt Noel teased.

"As a matter of fact, I think I'd better," Mark replied. "How about it, Vicki? If you must go out with this — this person, at least let Holly and me go along. Make it a double date."

"Sure, Mark," Vicki said. "Holly's a swell gal; we'll have fun."

Aunt Noel guided the conversation to more pleasant topics, and when their dinner was over Vicki performed her evening chores with her mind half on her work and half on her date with Penni. She wanted to get along with Mark, but she refused to let him manage her private life. After all that had been said about Penni, she was rather glad that their evening was going to include another couple. But perhaps she could show Mark that his low opinions were completely unreasonable and that Penni was a gentleman.

Chapter Seven

On Wednesday nights the Reef Royal dining patio catered to hotel guests as well as to their friends, and Vicki found no moments for relaxation until dessert time. After serving the cook's mouth-watering poha chiffon pie to the last table in her section, she refilled coffee cups, then strolled to the edge of the *lanai* to rest for a moment. A flickering light caught her eye, and she saw Buzz crossing the lawn. He was dressed in a short green hip sarong knotted loosely at his waist and was carrying a flaming torch.

The dining area was whisper silent as the guests watched the hypnotic scene. Buzz strolled at his usual care-free pace, and one by one lighted the black, conical shaped torches which were supported on six-foot standards and arranged in groups of three at inconspicuous spots on the hotel grounds.

It could have been a ritual from a thousand years ago, and its pagan beauty left Vicki speechless. The fanning winds whipped the orange flames, and the lawn was a mosaic of flickering light and shadows. Buzz disappeared for a moment then returned bearing a king-size conch. As he blew into one end of the shell, an eerie keening signaled the closing of the dining area.

Vicki was so mesmerized by the glowing torches and the wailing conch that she momentarily forgot about her evening date. But once the diners drifted from the *lanai* she realized that she'd have to rush if she were to finish her chores and be dressed by the time Penni arrived. Vicki frowned as she admitted that little by little she was falling into Holly's hurry-scurry habits.

The needle spray of a quick, cool shower relaxed and refreshed her, and as she stood at her closet studying her meager selection of dresses she wished she'd taken time to go shopping. But greeting Penni in an island costume was out of the question now. Slipping into an azure sheath, sleeveless and unbelted, she started to fasten a matching necklace around her neck. But as she caught sight of her reflection in the mirror, she dropped the jewelry back into its box. Greg had given her the necklace as a birthday gift, and the last time she'd worn this dress was on a date with him. Vicki felt a twinge of guilt as she hurried back to the closet to make another selection.

As she stood debating, Holly tapped on the door and poked her red head into the room. She'd added several inches to her height with an upswept hairdo, but before Vicki could comment, Holly spoke.

"Hey, you look great! Mark and I are waiting on the front *lanai*. Snap along, will you?"

"Be right there," Vicki said. Then, since Holly had seen her in the blue dress, she decided to wear it after all. Any change now might make Holly suspect this date with Penni was far more important than it really was.

"It's finished, completed, typed, and entered." Perching on a chair arm, Holly gestured and spoke to Mark and Buzz as Vicki joined them on the porch.

"That sounds fairly final." Vicki eased into a rattan rocker, a bit embarrassed to think Penni would find her waiting when he arrived. "But what are you talking about, Holly?"

Mark looked down at her without smiling. "Holly's the favored contender for Lili's scholarship, Vicki. She's won honorable mention for the two past summers, her stories have been anthologized, and this time I think she's really *in*."

"Swell!" Vicki said. "I'd like to read your stories sometime."

"Are you positive you don't write?" Holly impaled Vicki with her gaze and observed her as a scientist might study an intriguing specimen. "You're not holding out on us, are you?"

"I do keep a journal — a sort of daily record of ideas and impressions," Vicki said, "and I'd love to write real stories, but I've just never done it. What on earth would I write about?"

"If you have to ask, you'll never know." Mark stalked away from them.

"Why don't you set down some of the stories you told me years ago when we visited you on the mainland?" Buzz asked.

Had he really remembered those tales of hers, Vicki wondered, looking gratefully at Buzz. Beneath his clowning and teasing was a kindness that seemed inborn in Hawaiians, at least in the ones whom Vicki had met so far. She knew that Buzz's suggestion was designed to foil Mark's stinging comment.

"Did you really like those silly yarns?" Vicki asked.

"You'd better believe it." Buzz grinned. "My favorite was the one about the boy who lost a giraffe."

"Were they your own stories?" Holly asked.

Vicki nodded. "I made them up to entertain the neighborhood children when I did babysitting."

"So, great!" Holly exclaimed. "Why not write one or two of the better ones down and let Lili have a peek. It might be the start you need to speed you to a new career. Use my typewriter if you need one, or maybe that portable's still at the back of Sue's closet."

Holly was so in earnest that Vicki couldn't help giving her words some serious thought. In her burning desire to write something great, she had overlooked the possibilities of setting down some of her simple oral stories that had made such a hit with the small fry in San Francisco.

She could write the giraffe tale easily enough. Perhaps she owed it to her parents as well as to herself to grab this opportunity to test her talent. She would be risking nothing but a few hours of her time. Far better to do that and to really learn what her writing aptitude was than to dream of marriage combined with a literary career or to gamble months and hundreds of dollars in college tuition sponsored by her family. Perhaps she could enter Lili's contest and still hide the fact that writing was all-important to her. It wouldn't be easy, but she could try.

Buzz and Holly had wafted fresh breezes through the mental windows that Lili had already opened in Vicki's mind. Vicki made her decision. She would write, she would enter Lili's contest, and she would begin in the first free hours of the following day.

Vicki was still bouncing the giraffe story about in her mind when Penni roared into the driveway at the wheel of a compact car. He waved to them and waited. Vicki caught Mark's look of disgust at Penni's rudeness, ignored it, and called good-bye to Buzz as she led the way across the *lanai*.

"Hi, Penni," Vicki said. "I've invited Mark and Holly Hastings to go along with us, okay?"

"Fine with me." Penni leaned across the front seat to open the door for Vicki.

"Nice car, Penni." Vicki slipped in beside him.

"My older brother's in the rental business," Penni said. "He loaned me this heap for tonight, but in a few days I'll have a car of my own. All I need is a little more loot for the down payment."

While Mark and Holly were crawling into the back seat, Penni pulled a slender white lei from a plastic bag, placed it around Vicki's neck, and gave her a quick kiss.

Vicki was confused and speechless. The

flowers were gorgeous, but she resented Penni's brashness.

"An approved custom in the islands." Holly leaned forward to touch one of the perfumed blossoms, and Vicki found reassurance in her voice. She remembered Buzz's greeting at the airport and regained her composure.

"Thank you, Penni." Vicki adjusted the lei and a jasmine-sweet scent filled the car. "What kind of flowers are these?"

"Pikake," Penni answered. "They were once favorites of Princess Kaiulani who also was fond of peacocks. The Hawaiians honored her by naming the blossoms pikake."

"I love flowers," Vicki said, " but it seems a shame to pick them only to have them wilt so soon."

"When they wilt I'll bring you fresh ones," Penni promised. "The islands are full of them."

Penni raced the motor, and as they sped from the driveway he waved at a pacing, white-clad figure on the Hale Maile lawn. Lafe Yankton glanced the other direction as if he hadn't seen them. As Vicki watched Penni's hands on the steering wheel she saw the angry burn seared deep into the flesh between his thumb and forefinger, and she remembered that he'd worn a bandage that afternoon at the beach.

"Penni, how did you hurt your hand?"

Penni turned his wrist to hide the burn. "It's nothing serious." He answered her with a finality that invited no questions, and they drove on several blocks toward Waikiki before he spoke again.

"Where would you like to go tonight, Vicki?"

"I really don't know." Vicki glanced into the back seat hoping for suggestions from Mark or Holly. "Any place will be exciting and different to me."

"How about a walk down Kalakaua Avenue?" Penni suggested. "That's always good for openers."

"Great," Vicki answered. "How about it? Mark? Holly?"

"Fine!" Holly agreed. "Mark and I love to window shop."

Mark's scowl warned Vicki that he thought Penni a cheapskate and that he hated window shopping, but Penni was already edging the car into a curbside parking slot.

They joined thronging tourists and servicemen who were spending their evening on Kalakaua, and Vicki was delighted at all she saw. Many stores were open. Inside their flood-lighted interiors were exhibited everything from muumuus, aloha shirts, and brightly-flowered beachwear to Oriental paintings, hand-carved furniture, and cheap souvenirs. They strolled past several hotels and a wax museum, then Penni paused at the rustic entrance to the International Market Place.

"Here's where I work." He nodded toward some open thatch-roofed shops inside a large, wood-fenced compound.

"I thought you worked at the Coral Towers," Vicki said.

"True." Penni grinned. "But two nights a week I perform here as part of a Polynesian program for the tourists."

"I'd love to see you sometime," Vicki said. "What do you do?"

"I'll show you tomorrow night at seven. How about it?" Penni touched her elbow and guided her past a Japanese garden and fish pond and on toward an ice-cream stand.

"Gee, Penni, I can't make it that early. I work at Reef Royal until after the dining area closes."

"I'll trade duties with you tomorrow," Holly said, overhearing their conversation. "You serve breakfast for me, I'll do dinner duty for you. Everyone should see this show — it's the greatest."

"Keep out of it." Mark warned Holly in an undertone audible only to the three of them.

Vicki's anger flared at Mark's unfair and highhanded manner. "It's a deal, Holly. Penni, I can be ready any time you say."

Penni claimed a deserted table on a starlit terrace where they sipped coconut malts as they watched the milling crowd. Only when Holly was eating did she seem to relax.

"Sometimes the visitors put on a better show than the natives." Mark glanced at a brassy-haired, heavyset matron in a flopping palm-frond hat and a wildly flowered shortie muumuu who was walking barefoot along the asphalt path.

"Let's not knock the tourists, Chum." Penni grinned at Mark. "Hawaii needs them; besides, they're harmless."

"They may be the biggest business since sugar cane," Mark said, "but what a pain! For ten days they strut in muumuus and aloha shirts, stuff themselves on pineapple, and dip their inexperienced fingers into poi bowls at commercial luaus, but when back on the mainland they won't even remember the names of the islands they visited. What a bunch of phonies!"

"Mark! How unfair!" Vicki blurted out the words, then chewed her tongue to keep from telling Mark what a boor she thought he was.

"I feel sorry for them," Penni said.

"Why feel sorry?" Holly asked. "They're having a small ball."

"But sooner or later tourists have to go home," Penni said.

"Wouldn't you like to go to the mainland?" Vicki asked.

"Not for more than a vacation," Penni answered. "Hawaii will always be my home. Anyone lucky enough to be born here would be a fool to leave."

"So you're content to spend your life catering to the tourists!" Mark's voice was icy, and Vicki knew he was resenting his enforced duty at Reef Royal. Penni could feel sorry for the tourists if he wanted to, but Vicki decided to save her sympathy for Mark. She wished she could think of some way to help him overcome his fear of responsibility.

"How about a drive, Vicki?" Penni ignored Mark's ill humor and rude manners, and Vicki admired his self-control as she nodded in consent.

"Where shall we go?" Holly asked as they left the Market Place and retraced their steps along Kalakaua.

Penni didn't answer, but he threaded a

path through the crowd, and when they were back in the car he swung out into traffic and headed toward the mountains. As they sped along a sweeping highway Mark leaned forward.

"Where're you taking us, Penni?"

"Thought I'd show Vicki the Nuuanu Valley."

"Well, don't go too far in this car," Mark warned.

Penni ignored Mark's words, stomped the accelerator, and grinned like an imp at Vicki. "Ever seen the Pali?"

Vicki shook her head.

"Stop the car!" Mark ordered. "You must be some kind of a nut to consider driving up there tonight! Let us out and we'll hitch a ride back to town."

"Calm it, Mark." Penni's knife-edged tone sliced through Mark's protest. "I've been up this road thousands of times. I know my way around."

"What is this Pali?" Vicki asked. "Is it dangerous?"

"It'll be murder in *this* car," Mark said. "The Pali's a cliff-like break in the mountain wall where gales from windward Oahu whip through to the leeward side of the island. No one in his right mind drives a compact up there."

Penni was still grinning, and Vicki was inclined to join him. It surprised her that Mark was so full of fears. She couldn't imagine an ordinary wind strong enough to endanger an automobile. After all, they weren't driving into a tornado or a hurricane — why, this valley was peaceful as the Reef Royal lawn.

"Close the starboard windows," Penni said. "Here we go to the top."

Vicki gasped when she felt the car shudder as the wind slapped it broadside, but Penni gunned to the top of the incline and parked with the front bumper grazing a lava-rock retaining wall. He jumped from the car and motioned for Vicki to slide under the steering wheel and join him.

"Stay here," Mark said. "Penni's trying to make a fool of you."

"Come on, Vicki." Penni reached for her hand. "You'll never have such an experience again."

Vicki gripped Penni's hand for support and left Mark and Holly in the car. She had never known so wild a wind; it sucked her very breath away. While the gale pasted her hair to her head and moulded her sheath to her body, she snatched from it the odor of jasmine. Her lei danced about her neck like a live thing. Vicki peered over the retaining wall just long enough to comprehend the magnitude of the precipice. Suddenly she was frightened.

"Enough!" Seeming to sense her fear, Penni led Vicki back to the car. When they had caught their breath, he drove back into the hushed valley, and it was impossible to believe that such a howling wind raged only a few miles above them. Holly made an attempt at conversation, but Mark nursed a sullen silence and left the car without so much as a thank you when Penni stopped in front of Reef Royal.

"It's been a wonderful evening, Penni," Vicki said. "Thank you so much."

"See you tomorrow," Penni reminded as he zoomed away.

Vicki watched the car disappear from the driveway, and when she turned both Holly and Mark had left her. She went to her room, stood in front of her mirror, and attacked her blonde hair with a stout brush. Even so, it was several minutes before she could unsnarl the wind-driven tangles. Vicki hung her blue dress on its hanger and thought of Greg — that boy she'd known a million years ago on some other planet. She must write to Greg — tomorrow.

As Vicki dropped into bed she remembered her anxiety about Mark and all his fear and bitterness, and she wondered how Holly managed to put up with such behavior. Holly was pretty and pleasant; she could have her choice of boyfriends.

Vicki inhaled the fragrance of the pikake lei which she had draped over a chair back, and although she tried to ban him from her mind, Penni kept stealing into her thoughts. She felt guilty at having had such a good time with someone other than Greg. But that was silly; she and Greg had agreed to date others. Still, Vicki hadn't known that there were boys like Penni Pulianano.

On the surface Penni seemed like an easygoing, docile Hawaiian, but tonight at the Pali, his glittering black eyes and daring actions had suggested that his veneer of gentility hid a wildness as relentless as the raging Pali winds. Vicki suspected that Mark was right — that the Nuuanu Pali was unsafe for lightweight cars.

Was it only three days ago that Vicki felt so sure that a trip to the islands would provide her with two months of respite from making important decisions? What a joke! Her mind was teetering with decisions. What should she do to help Mark? Should she date Penni again? The only thing she was sure about was that she intended to enter Lili's contest.

Aunt Noel was trusting her to do the right thing where Penni was concerned, but she was confused. How could she be almost-engaged to one boy and still look forward to the company of another?

Vicki felt oddly depressed. She'd battled her parents and compromised her own soul to tie up that bundle of decisions she'd thought were stored in San Francisco. But somehow a string had slipped; the bundle was leaking, and only she could replenish it. Vicki felt as if her brain were draped with a lei of prickly, perplexing questions.

Chapter Eight

The alarm clock jangled like a fire bell, and Vicki fumbled to shut it off, then forced herself to get out of bed. The day promised to be a busy one, and she had some personal chores to do before reporting for breakfast detail.

After running a comb through her hair and slipping into her blue robe, she sat down at the desk and dragged out stationery and pen.

"Dear Greg," . . . What a doddering beginning! Vicki's mind strayed from the letter as she chewed the pliant end of the ball point. Perhaps some fresh air would stimulate her brain. Opening the sliding doors wide, she stepped out onto the *lanai*.

The Reef Royal grounds exuded smiling, tropical serenity, but farther inland wind and lightning lashed the mountains. Somehow the scene reminded her of Mark, whose outer calmness guarded an inner storm of passions. Vicki dreaded meeting her cousin this morning. Although she'd found her date with Penni fascinating and exciting, she knew that Mark considered the evening a fiasco, and she could feel his disapproval like a scratchy wool cloak about her shoulders.

Vicki returned to her room and once again sat down to write her letter. This time the words flowed like water and she filled two pages on both sides. Only when she re-read her message did she notice that she'd given a detailed resume of her brief stay in Honolulu without once mentioning Penni. And although she wished it otherwise, Penni Pulianano was the morning headline in her mind. Sighing, Vicki placed the letter in its envelope, and propped it against the pink conch-shell desk lamp where she would be sure to see it and remember to take it to the mail drop.

In the few minutes remaining before breakfast duty Vicki poked into the recesses of Sue's closet. There, as Holly had suggested was a portable typewriter. Vicki lifted the slim gray case into the bedroom, dusted it off, then plunked it onto the desk. Ripping a sheet of paper from the back of her journal, she rolled it in the machine and typed the title in all caps: "THE BOY WHO LOST A GIRAFFE." That much was easy — sort of like "Dear Greg," she thought.

Vicki recalled the story plot easily enough, but setting it down in words and sentences was another matter. Where did one begin? Trying to write something worthwhile was an awesome and frustrating endeavor. Vicki stared at the blank page until almost time to go to work. By hurrying into her clothes she managed to squeeze out a minute for bed making, but she left the typewriter on the desk. Perhaps she'd have time to put the story on paper later in the morning.

Once the day's routine started, it swept Vicki along like a piece of driftwood caught in a rip tide. Duty followed duty like endless waves breaking on the shore, but when her morning work was finished Vicki was surprised to find that she had almost an hour-and-a-half break before lunch. Writing time. Stretching out on her bed she mentally tried to compose the first few paragraphs of her story, but the next thing she knew, someone was tapping on her door and she heard Buzz's voice.

"Lunch time, Vicki," he said.

"Oh, Buzz!" Startled, Vicki jumped up and opened the door. "Am I late?"

"A little, but I covered for you." Buzz noticed the typewriter. "Decide to enter a story in Lili's contest?"

Vicki scowled. "I may, Buzz. I may, if I can get past the title." Closing her door, she followed Buzz to the dining area. From across the porch she saw Mark's disapproving glance, but she pretended not to notice and went on with her duties.

"I enjoyed sleeping late for a change," Holly said as they worked across from each other at the buffet table. Then she lowered her voice and leaned her head close to Vicki. "Mark was sore because I encouraged you to go with Penni tonight, Vicki. Hope nothing happens to prove he's right and I'm wrong."

"It's none of Mark's affair, but I'll see that everything goes well. Sometimes Mark has very disturbing ideas. I wondered, were you scared at the Pali?"

"Sort of," Holly said. "Sometimes officers patrol that road and turn back all lightweight cars. Penni was foolish to risk brushing into real trouble. But since we all survived, I think we should forget about the whole thing."

There was no chance for more conversation; the luncheon guests were drifting toward the flower studded buffet table. Vicki was glad when everyone was seated and some of the hub-bub died down. She was helping Buzz refill water glasses when Lili

Lanuoka and her two friends appeared to sing. Smiling like pleased children, the ladies left the *lanai* and performed their music under the branches of the banyan tree on the back lawn. They had finished "Little Grass Shack" and were beginning "Sailing Along the Wailua River" when Vicki felt a touch on her elbow. Turning, she looked down into the dark eyes of the tiny Japanese girl who had delivered the box of orchids on Vicki's first day of duty.

"Hello, Miniki." Vicki was glad she remembered the girl's name, because Miniki appeared frightened and ill at ease. " Can I help you?"

"Please, Missy, I must speak to Mrs. Wong."

"She's entertaining right now," Vicki said. "She'll be finished in a few minutes. Would you care to wait?"

"Please, Missy, I must see her right away. Already she is angry with me."

Vicki looked around the dining area for her aunt, hoping that she would deal with Miniki. But too late! Mrs. Wong had spotted her prey. The other two queenly Hawaiians continued singing as if nothing had happened until Buzz sauntered over to join them. Vicki wanted to listen to Buzz's song, but Miniki clutched at her arm.

Mrs. Wong was striding toward them with the jutting jaw and determined eye of an angered marlin, and Vicki whisked Miniki to a corner of the *lanai* away from the dining guests.

"Miniki!" Mrs. Wong's resonant voice matched her out-size physical proportions. "Where are my vandas and frangipani? How do I keep in business if you don't deliver the blossoms that I order? This is the number two time you've been late this week."

"Please, Mrs. Wong, forgive me," Miniki said. "My cart has a broken wheel and I abandoned the flowers in the valley."

Before Mrs. Wong could scold anymore, Vicki spoke up. "Let's tell Aunt Noel. Perhaps she'll let Mark go get the flowers in the Reef Royal car."

Vicki ran to find her aunt, but she still heard Mrs. Wong's threats to refuse any blossoms that were wilted. Seeing Aunt Noel at the lobby desk, Vicki quickly outlined the problem.

"Of course, we must help," Aunt Noel agreed. "Mrs. Wong needs the blossoms for her lei shop; Miniki needs Mrs. Wong's business. Miniki supports an invalid grandmother by selling flowers, and she works long and hard to bring them into the city from their small acre in the valley. Can you drive, Vicki?"

"Yes, Aunt Noel. But I've never driven in Honolulu traffic."

"It shouldn't be any worse than the traffic on your San Francisco hills." Aunt Noel laughed. "Take Miniki and Mrs. Wong with you; they'll show you the way." She handed Vicki a ring of keys. "The car's in the south parking lot."

Vicki hurried to tell Miniki and Mrs. Wong that the flowers were as good as rescued, but Mrs. Wong was still upset.

"The blossoms will be wilted by now," she said. "I will lose a day's sales because of you, Miniki."

"I pulled the cart off the road into deep shade," Miniki said. "Let us go see the true condition of the flowers."

"Wait a sec." Vicki dashed to the kitchen and returned with several large pans filled with ice. Handing one container to Mrs. Wong and another to Miniki, she carried the third one herself and paused at the lobby desk to beg some aspirin from her aunt.

"A headache, Vicki?"

"No." Vicki smiled. "At our florist shop back home Daddy sometimes dissolves aspirin in water to lengthen the life of cut flowers. I thought I'd try it on Miniki's blossoms."

"Fine idea," Aunt Noel called as they hurried toward the car. "And good luck!"

Sitting in the front seat with Vicki, Miniki directed her toward the winding street where the wooden flower cart minus one wheel was hopelessly stalled. Vicki pulled the car off the road, and the three of them hurried over to the abandoned cart. Although the day was pleasantly cool, Vicki had turned the car air conditioner to high speed and now she left the car motor running while they transferred the lavender and pink blossoms from the cart to the containers of ice water. How bad the damage? The orchids were in fairly good condition. The frangipani? Mrs. Wong was still noncommittal about accepting them.

"Where to now?" Vicki asked.

"To my stand on Kalakaua Avenue," Mrs. Wong said. "I saw you pass last night, but you were on the other side of the street."

"I would have stopped to see you had I known your stand was so near," Vicki said.

"I'll stay and help you string the leis," Miniki volunteered. "And tomorrow I will be on time. That is a solemn promise."

Vicki purposely drove slowly, and after a few minutes in the chilling air of the car the flowers began to freshen. By the time they reached Mrs. Wong's thatch-roofed shack, Miniki had removed and discarded any badly wilted blossoms.

"You will accept the flowers, Mrs. Wong?" Miniki asked.

"Yes, yes." Mrs. Wong's attitude changed completely. "Thanks to Vicki and Noel Foster I'll be able to open my stand as usual. If you'll help me make up the leis you can continue to count on my business."

Vicki could almost feel Miniki relax, and when they parked the car, Miniki hurried to carry the flowers to Mrs. Wong's cramped sidewalk shop. Staying to watch the lei-stringing process, Vicki ended up spending part of her afternoon threading the fragrant pink frangipani, which she discovered was another name for plumeria, on woven white fiber and tying the finished lengths into leis.

As the three of them worked together, Mrs. Wong grew cheerful, and Vicki couldn't resist questioning her about Lili's intended departure from Reef Royal. Surely this girlhood friend would know Lili's reason for moving to Hale Maile. For once Vicki determined to be cautious and subtle and not to blurt out her most important question first.

"Mrs. Wong, do you know how Reef

115

Royal got its name? I've been meaning to ask Aunt Noel, but I really haven't had a chance."

Mrs. Wong didn't look up from her work. "Coral reefs surround all the islands, Vicki, but in ancient times preferred beaches were reserved for the royal family. The beach area that you can see from your aunt's hotel was at one time *kapu,* or forbidden, to the common people. As far as I know that's where the idea for the name originated."

"And what about Hale Maile across the street?" Vicki prided herself on easing into the subject that interested her most.

"*Hale* means house," Mrs. Wong said. "Maile is a green foliage vine with a spicy-woodsy fragrance. Maile leis are still favorites of older Hawaiians, but the vine is hard to find these days. Such leis are reserved for state occasions."

"When Lili moves to Hale Maile I'll miss your singing," Vicki began.

"We all love to sing." Mrs. Wong hung a round vanda lei on a display hook. "But Buzz sings well. Perhaps he will fill our spot."

"Mrs. Wong, tell me. *Why* is Lili leaving Aunt Noel?" Vicki asked the question she had been leading up to and waited breathlessly for the answer. Mrs. Wong looked at her from eyes glistening with unshed tears and shook her head.

"I am not free to say, child. It is between Lili and . . ." Her voice choked up. "I am not free to say."

Chapter Nine

Vicki drove back to Reef Royal, parked the car under an African tulip tree whose flaming blossoms glowed like an altar fire, and sat for a moment deep in thought. If someone at the hotel had offended Lili, why didn't she speak up and try to right the misunderstanding? No, Vicki thought, Lili's moving had to be prompted by a reason more important than wounded feelings. But what could it be? Mrs. Wong knew the answer, yet it was obvious that she planned to keep Lili's secret.

Dropping the car keys off at the lobby desk, Vicki paused long enough to assure her aunt that they had saved Miniki's flowers, then she went to her bedroom to work on her story. This time she quit straining to write impressive, spangled prose and she put the tale down simply, as if she were telling it to please some favorite child back in San Francisco. With this goal in mind the words flowed more freely. When she finished, she was pleased to see four and a half typed pages.

Rolling the final sheet from the type-writer, Vicki carried the manuscript to an easy chair on her *lanai* and began proof-reading, making corrections, and penciling in revisions. She had worked almost two hours when Mark stormed across the lawn and stood before her with hands on hips and eyes blazing sparks.

"Whatever is wrong, Mark?"

Mark denounced her with his stare for an-other moment. "Thanks to *you,* Lili's moving first thing Monday morning."

"Impossible!" Vicki's voice dropped to a whisper. "But that's only three days away."

Mark nodded. "And worse yet, she's ad-vancing the deadline for contest entries to Saturday midnight and will announce the winner following Sunday afternoon's buffet. Our writing guests will be wild when they see her announcement on the bulletin board, Vicki. What put it into your head to pump Mrs. Wong? Why'd you do it?"

So that's what had happened! Vicki felt exposed and as bare inside as an abandoned sea shell when she realized that Mrs. Wong must have warned Lili that the Fosters were prying into her private affairs.

"Mark, I really thought I could help." Vicki tried to swallow the bitter taste that suddenly coated her tongue like the dregs of a sickening medicine. "We can't hope to keep Lili at Reef Royal unless we know her reason for leaving."

"Well, your scheme backfired." As Mark turned and stomped off toward the dining area, Vicki trudged to the lobby to talk to her aunt.

"Mark just told me the horrid news, Aunt Noel. I don't know what to say or do. It's all my fault."

"Mark is none too tactful, Vicki. Don't blame yourself so." Aunt Noel sighed. "Lili intended to move soon. A few days one way or the other won't make much difference."

In the silence Vicki heard a dove call and found the flower-scented air almost cloying in its sweetness. How could she possibly notice such trivial things when so important an issue faced her!

"Do the guests know yet?" Vicki eyed the foreboding notice on the bulletin board.

"Only a few."

"And they've cancelled their reservations." Vicki guessed the worst from her aunt's evasive answer. "What can I do, Aunt Noel?"

Her aunt patted her on the shoulder. "Vicki, how about delivering Lili's coffee tray? I feel certain that her decision is final, but at least you can make sure there are no hard feelings between the two of you before she goes."

Vicki took refuge in the kitchen, and all the time she was preparing the snack she searched her mind for some way to atone for her presumptuous idea of questioning Mrs. Wong.

When she knocked at the apartment, Lili greeted her as if nothing unusual had happened, but Vicki was too upset to face a half-hour's meaningless chitchat, and as soon as she was seated on the bamboo couch she hauled the terrible subject to the surface of their conversation as if it were an evil monster dredged from the depths of the sea.

"Lili, I'm terribly sorry if I upset you by asking Mrs. Wong your reason for moving. Really, I was trying to help you and the Fosters."

"I understand." Lili's eyes held an unfathomable expression, a combination of sadness, dignity, and compassion. "But I must go. There is no other way. You only made me realize how unfair I was being by prolonging my departure. How much better to make a swift, clean break! I was only pampering myself by waiting until the last possible moment to move."

Last possible moment before what, Vicki

wondered. But Lili gave her no more opportunities for either questions or apologies.

"Vicki, I had hoped you would bring your journal with you today. Surely you'll change your mind and let me see it."

After what she'd done, Vicki felt she had no choice but to grant Lili's wish. "Of course, Lili. Excuse me a moment and I'll get it for you."

Vicki hurried to her room, grabbed the battered notebook from under her sketch pad, and returned to Lili's apartment.

"Here it is, Lili." Vicki handed the journal to her hostess.

"Let's make a trade," Lili said. "I'll read a bit of your journal while you glance at one of my features in the *Gazette*." She thrust a yellowed sheaf of newspapers at Vicki.

For awhile Vicki only pretended to read, all the time watching Lili's face for some sign of approval or disapproval of the journal. But Lili's face remained expressionless.

Giving up her vigil, Vicki scanned one feature under Lili's byline and was impressed with the clarity with which her personality came through in her writing. The article concerned ancient Hawaiian gods, and while it discussed their mysteries with a child-like simplicity, it also cloaked them in fine Hawaiian dignity. When Vicki finished reading about Kane, the father-mother of all living things; about Lono, the god of peace; and about Pele, the fire goddess, she felt not only an empathy for the ancient Polynesians, but also a new respect for Lili as a literary figure. When at last the noble lady looked up from the journal, Vicki was very eager to hear her opinion of her daily entries.

"Your writing shows talent, Vicki." Lili closed the notebook. "Writing is comprised of both talent and craftmanship. You have the former; the latter can be learned."

"Thank you, Lili. I'm working on a manuscript for your contest which I hope will please you. But now I must go. Thank you for letting me read your work. I like it very much. I wish . . ." Vicki hesitated. She'd been about to wish that Lili would help her learn the craft of writing, but under the circumstances that was impossible.

"I wish I could write as well as you do, Lili," she finished lamely, hardly able to believe that Lili had said she had talent. Vicki felt a real sense of loss as she realized that these chats with Lili would end when Lili left Reef Royal.

Returning the snack tray to the kitchen Vicki considered skipping dinner in her aunt's room. But that was out of the question. Much as she dreaded to, she knew she must face the family and Mark's open disapproval.

It was a quiet meal with Buzz and Aunt Noel trying to maintain a pleasant conversation in spite of Mark's glowering silence. Vicki had no appetite, but she ate from habit and felt as if the food turned to lava rock as it touched her stomach.

When the dinner ended Vicki headed for the kitchen before remembering that Holly was working the dinner shift for her. This afternoon she had wished that she could break her date with Penni, but now she was eager to see the Polynesian show. Perhaps it would give her an idea for a similar entertainment that the Fosters could stage at Reef Royal — an entertainment that would attract guests when Lili left them.

Showering quickly, Vicki slipped into the first dress in sight and vowed that she would be pleasant. After all, the troubles at Reef Royal weren't Penni's fault.

A few minutes before seven Penni made his entrance in a pink and white striped jeep with a canvas-canopy top. The vehicle looked so gay, so amusing that Vicki smiled in spite of herself. She slid onto the seat beside Penni and they drove toward Waikiki stopping at last in a parking lot filled with rental jeeps and cars.

"My brother's joint," Penni said. "International Market Place's about a block from here." He headed for the sidewalk before Vicki was even out of the jeep, but she caught up, then hurried to match his racing pace.

"Are we late, Penni?"

He nodded. "But I've arranged for a friend to save you a seat." Penni walked even faster. "I'll have to rush to get into costume."

Vicki was glad when they reached the Polynesian Review area so she could slow down. Penni led her through a performer's entrance behind the thatch-roofed stage, said a few rushed words to a boy about his own age who waited in the audience, then disappeared into the crowd without performing any introductions. Vicki had supposed that Penni's friend would watch the program with her, but instead, the boy gave her his place on the narrow green bench and left her alone.

Vicki glanced around. Although Penni lacked certain refinements, he had secured her an excellent seat. She sat to the front and center, and while some four or five hundred people pressed close by, at least that many more crowded the standing-room-only section.

The crowd gasped as the conch shells keened, and although the sound was familiar, Vicki felt a tingling excitement. Presently she saw Penni wearing a crimson hip sarong and leading a procession of five performers down the narrow aisle between the rows of seats. Behind him walked three barefoot Hawaiian girls whose shimmering black hair flowed to their waists and whose green-ti-leaf skirts and yellow frangipani leis were bathed in wavering shadows from the lighted torches they carried. At the rear of the procession marched another boy dressed like Penni, who was also sounding a conch shell.

Vicki was pleased. So far she had seen nothing that was beyond the talents of the Reef Royal employees. Idly she wondered how she and Holly would look in ti-leaf skirts. And would they need wigs?

When the stage show started Vicki was surprised to learn that the Hawaiian hula is a graceful dance in which a story is told by the movements of the dancer's hands and arms. Vicki tucked this information into her memory for future use. The performers made many costume changes, sometimes dancing in ti-leaf skirts, sarongs, and holomuus, but it wasn't until the frenzied Tahitian hula began that Vicki saw the grass skirt that is so often mentioned and copied on the mainland.

Vicki made mental notes of all she heard and saw, trying to telescope the whole program to proportions suitable for Reef Royal, and she was so carried away by the stories and costumes that she forgot all about Penni until she heard a murmur ripple through the crowd. Penni stepped on stage brandishing a long-handled knife which gleamed and flashed in the torchlight. His eyes glittered with the bold, wild spark she had noticed at the Pali, and Vicki held her breath.

That can't be a real knife, she thought as Penni whirled and dipped, twirling and tossing the streaking weapon like a drum major's baton. The crowd applauded, gasped, and applauded again and again. At the end of his performance Penni demonstrated the knife's sharpness by slicing a tough-skinned pineapple with quick, snapped strokes and tossing the chunks of golden dripping fruit to the shouting children who crowded at the edge of the stage.

As soon as the program ended, the audience dispersed quickly, and Vicki sat alone on the empty bench. When at last Penni returned, he was dressed in street clothes, and his face showed no signs of make-up.

"You were great, Penni," Vicki said. "I was scared to death you'd accidentally amputate something."

Penni basked in her praise as he led the way toward the ice-cream bar they had visited the night before.

"Wait here a minute." Without excusing himself, Penni abandoned her on the pathway as he dashed a few steps ahead to accost a fat, white-clad stranger. Although she couldn't see the man's face, Vicki knew from his clothes and his size that he must be Lafe Yankton. At first she paid no attention, but as the talk grew animated, she sensed an argument. *Come on, Penni,* Vicki thought. She wanted no trouble with the Fosters' competitor, and although she didn't intend to listen to the conversation, Penni's voice rose and she couldn't help hearing.

"Ten bucks." Penni's usually smooth voice was coarse and hard as rough lava.

"Later," Lafe answered.

"Now." Penni insisted.

Vicki was surprised to see Lafe Yankton reach for his wallet, fish out a bill, and hand it to Penni.

"Not a cent more until . . ." Lafe's voice faded, and Penni returned to Vicki's side with a smirking grin. "No more ice-cream stands for us," he said. "Let's try Duke Kahanamoku's for a bite to eat."

"I've heard that name somewhere," Vicki said.

"The Duke was a champion surfer in his day," Penni replied. "The greatest! And his place is neat — strictly class."

Inside the dimly lighted restaurant a hostess led them to a table for two where a candle glowed from deep inside a red globe encased in umber fish netting. While they waited for their order to arrive, Penni entertained her with tales of his own feats on the surfboard, and although Vicki knew that both Mark and Greg would consider her date a braggart, she was glad that all she had to do was to smile and to listen.

Penni talked during their whole meal as well as during their walk back to the parking lot, and it wasn't until they were in the jeep and heading out toward Diamond Head that Vicki spoke.

"Where are we going, Penni?"

"Thought I'd show you the blow hole," he answered.

"What's that?" Vicki asked, although she had too much on her mind to be really interested in the local scenery.

"It's an unusual lava formation," Penni

said. "All these islands are the tops of mountains built up from the ocean floor by volcanic eruptions, you know."

"No, I didn't know," Vicki said. "You wouldn't be teasing me, would you? How could all these flowers and trees grow in lava rock?"

"Over the years the wind, sun and rain change the rock into soil." Penni honked the horn and passed a black Ford. "Vegetation begins to appear about five to ten years after an eruption."

"You mean there're still active volcanoes in the islands?" Vicki asked.

"Sure!" Penni pulled the jeep off the highway and into a moon-washed observation area. "Here on Oahu the Diamond Head and Koko Head craters have slept for millions of decades, but over on the big island of Hawaii the Mauna Loa erupts about every three years, and the Kilauea volcano puffs steam most of the time." Penni edged closer to Vicki and pointed straight ahead. "Look! There goes the blow hole!"

Vicki watched as a streak of water like a white plume spouted skyward then splashed into a seething froth against the jagged rocks.

"It looks like a geyser," Vicki said.

"It's caused by the tide rushing under a

lava-rock shelf and forcing the ocean up through the small opening. There it goes again." Penni dropped his arm around Vicki's shoulder, and to avoid him she slipped out of the jeep.

"I'd like a closer look," she said, hoping she hadn't offended him.

Penni followed her to an iron guard railing, and they stood in the moonlight gazing at the pounding ocean. Almost every incoming wave agitated the blow hole, and Vicki tasted salt on her lips as the trade winds blew a misty spray into her face. Penni took her hand and started back to the jeep.

"This is a beautiful spot, Penni. Really much nicer than the Pali." They both laughed, remembering their struggle with the raging wind. "But I have to go home early tonight," Vicki said. "I'm entering Lili Lanuoka's creative writing competition, and the manuscript deadline is midnight Saturday. I have scads of work to do on my story between now and then."

"You're not going to spoil our evening, are you?" Penni leaned forward and tried to pull Vicki toward him, but she pretended to search for a comb in her purse.

"Please, Penni! Let's don't argue!"

Penni gave a mocking laugh and slid back

under the steering wheel. "Ten bucks I spend, and now you want to get home early!" He started the jeep, bounced it back onto the highway, and tromped on the accelerator.

"Penni!" Vicki's mouth went dry. "Penni, be careful!"

Penni blasted his horn at a red station wagon, pulled out to pass, but instead of going on around, he drove alongside the vehicle and tried to goad the driver into a drag race.

"Penni, here comes a car!" Vicki screamed the words as headlights bore down upon them like two beacons. "We're going to crash!" Just as she thought there was no escaping a head-on smash-up, Penni jerked the jeep across the highway and toward the ocean. Vicki clutched the seat as they careened over ruts, rocks, and brush, then hit the beach. Penni raced the motor, the wheels spun in the loose sand, and Vicki seized her chance for escape.

Almost paralyzed with fright for her own safety, and swamped with guilt and remorse for going out with Penni against Mark's wishes, Vicki jumped from the jeep and dashed toward the glowing neon of a service station far back on the highway. Sand filled her shoes, and her lungs burned from the exertion of running, but she didn't panic. She was safe. The moon lighted her way, and as she reached the protection of the gasoline station she still could hear the spin of jeep tires against sand. Resting in the shadows until she caught her breath and stopped trembling, Vicki approached the attendant.

"May I help you, Ma'am?" the man asked.

Vicki blushed as she realized how she must look. "May I make a phone call, please?"

The attendant pointed to the telephone and politely left the room so she could talk in private.

After calling a cab, Vicki retired to the ladies' room to freshen up and to wait. How could she have been so gullible as to fall into a trap like this? Mark had tried to warn her. Even Aunt Noel had confidence in her ability to choose suitable friends. Vicki began to doubt her own judgment. First she'd made her parents unhappy by refusing to go to college, then she'd made trouble for everyone at Reef Royal by prying into private affairs, and now this made twice that she'd become involved with Penni and his dangerous, harebrained activities. Vicki felt as hollow inside as she had as a child when she'd done wrong and knew she was in for a spanking. Only this feeling was worse. She was on her own now. No one was going to mete out any punishment; she had to go on living with herself with no understanding of how she could atone for her mistakes.

It wasn't until she was in the taxi nearing Reef Royal that she remembered that Mark would be working at the lobby desk.

"Let me out at the driveway, please." Vicki leaned forward, mustered what dignity she could, and handed a bill to the cabbie. "And thank you so much!"

The taxi drove off, and Vicki waited for a moment before tip-toeing up the lane. She didn't want anyone to notice that she was coming in alone, and luck was on her side. Mark was engrossed in his typing and he merely nodded as she walked across the lobby and on to her room.

Earlier in the afternoon Vicki had had every intention of working on her story after her date with Penni, but the terrible, hectic evening had left her drained of energy and she could keep her mind on neither little boys nor lost giraffes. All the troubles at Reef Royal as well as the ones in her personal life churned through her head as she lay awake in bed long after she had turned out the light.

Just as she was dropping off to sleep Vicki

heard a strange noise at the sliding door which separated her room from the *lanai* and back lawn. She listened, but the sound wasn't repeated. Then, as she relaxed, it came again. There was no mistaking it. Someone was throwing pebbles against the glass. Who? Penni? Had he come to apologize?

Now alert, Vicki jumped from bed and slipped into her robe. If Penni was outside her door, she must send him away before Mark heard him. Mark would make a big thing of a midnight visitor, and Vicki had had enough big things for one day. Without opening the drapery she skinned behind it, silently opened the door, and peered into the moonlit night. She saw nothing and was about to return to bed when a tell-tale movement under the banyan tree caught her eye. Someone was lurking nearby.

Chapter Ten

Vicki peered into the shadows until she made out the form of Miniki standing beside one of the banyan's many aerial roots. Although silvery moonlight illumined the warm night Vicki shivered as she ran barefoot across the thick cool grass to the hidden spot where Miniki stood.

"What is it, Miniki? What on earth are you doing here at this time of night?" Miniki stood upright, but Vicki stooped uncomfortably to avoid twigs and leaves.

"Please, Missy, I want to repay your kindness. You helped me save my flowers this afternoon, now you must allow me the privilege of returning the favor."

Vicki almost laughed. She certainly could use some help. But from Miniki? Vicki doubted that this shy, fragile-appearing girl could aid her. "What do you have in mind, Miniki?"

"You desire to know why the *alii*, Lili, is leaving Reef Royal?"

"Do you know the reason?" Vicki

hunched closer to the Japanese girl. "Tell me, Miniki."

"To Mrs. Wong and Mrs. Hawagasa Lili confides all." Miniki whispered. "By accident I overheard them talking. It is a strange and chilling story gleaned from the ancient, pagan past. But I believe. The *alii*, Lili, speaks only the truth."

"Tell me, Miniki," Vicki said. "Tell me quickly, then I'll see if I may borrow the car to drive you back to the valley."

"No, no," Miniki said. "You must avoid my home at night. My grandmother would disapprove. I will return as I came, and she will never know that I've been gone."

"All right, Miniki, just tell me your story."

Miniki lowered her voice to the faintest of whispers. "The *alii*, Lili, fears the Marchers in the Night." Miniki had barely spoken when Vicki heard footsteps on the dining *lanai,* and looking up, she saw Mark pacing back and forth across the open porch.

Vicki pushed deeper into the shadows, but when she turned to warn Miniki, the girl was nowhere in sight. Suddenly Vicki was furious with herself. Mark might be prickly as a sea urchin, but it was her own fault that she let him put her constantly on the defensive. She wanted to rush from her hiding place. She wanted to inform him that it was absolutely none of his affair if she spent the whole night under the banyan tree.

But how useless! Mark hadn't even seen her. He had frightened Miniki away at a crucial moment, but clearly, he had only stepped outside to enjoy the peaceful evening. Vicki watched. Mark returned to the hotel lobby, slapped the grey plastic cover over his typewriter and dimmed the light.

"Miniki! Are you still here?" Vicki waited for an answer, for some revealing movement that would tell her the girl was still near. But no. Miniki was gone. When Vicki was sure she was alone, she padded back across the lawn to her room.

"The Marchers in the Night." She muttered the strange words like a magic chant as she tried to puzzle out their meaning, but the answer evaded her.

Even though Vicki was exhausted both mentally and physically, she couldn't sleep. She needed someone to talk with. But no one was awake at this hour except Mark, and she definitely didn't want his company. She missed Greg. Vicki wished he were here to apply his logical thinking to the maze of problems that baffled her. It would be comforting to be married to Greg, to know that one of them, at least, would be able to think his way out of puzzling situations. Well, she could talk to Greg on paper.

Bringing out her stationery Vicki began another letter, and this time she didn't try to imitate a tourist brochure. Instead she wrote a personal account of her visit including the problems involving Lili, Mark, Reef Royal, and even Penni Pulianano. When she finished she felt much better, and she slapped an airmail stamp on the blue envelope and took it to the lobby so it would go out first thing in the morning.

Throughout the night Vicki was half-conscious of sleeping fitfully — of tossing, of turning, and of dreaming, and when she awakened early Friday morning she turned to her contest story almost as a form of therapy. What does a person do when he can neither bear his problems nor solve them? Run away as Lili was going to do? Or turn grumpy and bitter like Mark?

Vicki blotted Penni Pulianano from her mind. If he had spent the night trying to free his brother's jeep from the sand, it was only what he deserved. It was no concern of hers. Her friendship with Penolo had ended.

Sitting at the desk, Vicki penciled more revisions on her original manuscript, then brought out fresh white bond and began to type the final copy. When she finished, the story looked short, insignificant, but she suddenly had the idea of including some sketched illustrations with it. Most children's stories were illustrated, weren't they? Perhaps some sketches might set her work apart from the many others Lili had read. But pictures would have to wait until later. Vicki was straightening her desk when Holly burst onto the *lanai* and popped her head into the room.

"How's the story coming along?" she asked.

"All right." Vicki offered Holly a chair, but she declined. "I still have some finishing touches to add, Holly, but I'll meet the new deadline."

"I've got to dash," Holly said. "I just stopped by to see if you had a good time with Penni last night."

"Oh, the Polynesian show was great." Vicki tried to evade Holly's question. "I'm going to ask Aunt Noel if we could put on a similar entertainment here — you know, something to attract guests after Lili leaves."

"Using what for talent?" Holly asked. "Buzz sings, but that's about it unless you've secretly learned to hula. Did Penni behave himself?"

"Say, Holly, have you ever heard anything about Hawaiian Marchers in the Night?"

Vicki tried again to distract Holly from the subject of Penolo Pulianano.

"Penni been cluing you in on island folklore?" Holly grinned.

Vicki didn't answer, and Holly continued. "I really know nothing about those old native legends and beliefs, but if Penni was feeding you tall tales, you can check on them at the public library on King Street. I have to dash now — breakfast time. See you later."

Vicki sighed her relief as Holly left, and she performed her own morning chores and noontime duties with only one thought in mind. She had to do some quick research. Slipping away from Reef Royal, she boarded a cream-colored bus and asked the driver to let her off at the library.

"Certainly, Ma'am," he replied. "New in the city?"

Vicki nodded as she deposited her fare.

"While you're in the vicinity you might enjoy seeing the Kamehameha statue and visiting Iolani Palace. They're all within walking distance of each other."

"Thank you, sir, I may do that." Vicki chose a seat near the front entrance and watched the passing scene through the window. Obligingly, the bus driver pointed out spots of interest, a Shinto temple, a

141

Buddhist temple, Chinatown, but when he announced her stop, Vicki stepped from the bus with no intention of visiting either statue or palace. She hurried directly to the stately library building.

A smartly dressed librarian helped Vicki find the books she needed, seeming to think nothing of the request. Vicki read. As the fascinating story of the Marchers in the Night unfolded, she thought of Lili. Surely this wise, dignified Hawaiian lady couldn't accept such fantasy as a vital part of her life. Vicki returned the book and walked outside as if in a daze. The bright sunshine and whispering palm fronds helped her turn off the macabre voices from the past, but a glance at her watch told her that she had many minutes to wait before the next bus stopped. She disliked being alone.

A short distance away the bronzed statue of Hawaii's great king shimmered in the sunlight. The black figure cloaked in a golden feather cape stood on a white masonry pedestal, and Vicki wished she knew more about Hawaiian history — real history, not folklore and superstitions. Time stood still. With minutes still to wait she followed a group of tourists who were heading toward an ornate gray building with many balconies enclosed by fancy iron railings.

"The only royal palace in the United States," one lady gushed to her husband.

"Royalty! Humph!" the man snorted. "I want to see the governor's office. The whole place serves as the State House now."

Vicki trailed behind the tourists as they crossed the street and stepped inside the low cement wall studded with iron shafts that rimmed the palace grounds. As she crossed the green lawn, a redbird darted like a crimson arrow from a high palm frond to the low-hanging branch of a Monkey Pod tree, and as the tourists stopped to watch it, Vicki walked on up the palace steps.

Inside the building a massive stairway rose from a central hall. Offices were open for inspection on either side of the staircase, but the prime attraction was the throne room where red plush draperies canopied two ornately carved seats. Vicki felt herself whisked to bygone times. The room seemed to try to speak as she visualized kings and queens reigning on their thrones beneath the high-paneled ceiling and crystal chandeliers. But ghosts? By no stretch of her imagination could Vicki picture shades of the ancient royalty marching in the night and speaking to their descendants.

Vicki left Iolani Palace without seeing the

governor's office. She preferred to remember the throne room and the gold-framed portraits of ancient kings that hung in the palace hallway. Perhaps these visions would make her more receptive to the story that she expected Lili Lanuoka to tell her.

Vicki arrived back at Reef Royal just in time to deliver Lili's coffee tray. Seated on Lili's bamboo sofa, Vicki drank a whole cup of strong Kona brew in order to steel herself to ask the questions that she must have answered.

"Lili," she began after they had exchanged a few pleasantries. "I'm neck-deep in trouble from my prying, but I think I know now why you're leaving Reef Royal. It's because of the Marchers in the Night, isn't it?"

Vicki traced the pattern in the pandanus floor mat nervously with one toe, wondering what kind of a response to expect from Lili. The question might goad her into moving that very day, or it might persuade her to talk about her problem and to let someone try to help her. At first the queenly lady remained silent, then she sighed and all the music left her voice.

"I don't know how or where you learned of this, Vicki, but the story must go no farther."

"Then it *is* true, isn't it?" Vicki persisted.

"Yes, it is true. But you must promise me that you will tell no one. My friends would ridicule me."

"You can trust me, Lili," Vicki said. "I'm not amused, and I'll tell no one who will laugh at you. But I'd like to know exactly what happened. Maybe I can help you."

Lili sighed again, and Vicki thought that her friend seemed to welcome telling her story to a sympathetic listener.

"Each evening at dusk it is my custom to exercise, to take a short walk across the rear lawn of Reef Royal and on into the paths and lanes of the unimproved area back of the hotel grounds. One future day this property will be landscaped into a city park, but right now we call this overgrown tangle of vegetation the jungle.

"It was on the Sunday night before you arrived that the ancient warriors appeared to me in this jungle. As a child I had heard tales of Marchers in the Night from my grandmother, from my great aunt, and from my parents, and at the time I never doubted their truth. But later my modern education refuted these folk-tales, and as I grew older I realized that the Night Marchers of which my relatives spoke must have been only illusions."

"Yet something changed your mind?" Vicki prompted.

"I tell you, I *saw* the marchers myself." Lili spoke in hushed tones. "I feel like a fool telling you this, but it was *not* my imagination. The marchers appeared to me — spoke to me. They wore the golden feather capes and helmets of the ancient *alii*, they carried royal feather staves, and all three bore candlenut torches. Yes, there were three of them, and they were as real as you are, Vicki. I wouldn't tell you this if it weren't true. I wouldn't believe it if I hadn't seen it."

"But you're still living," Vicki said. "According to the folklore I read this afternoon at the library, the marchers killed anyone who chanced to see them."

"That's an incomplete story," Lili said. "A person may see the marchers and be saved if he has an ancestor among the group to intercede for him. I was lucky. My family was of royal blood, and in this trio of marchers that I met was a warrior ancestor who remembered both my grandfather and my father. He persuaded his companions to spare me."

"What did he look like?" Vicki asked.

"He looked only slightly different from the others," Lili answered. "They were all young men, and this warrior who interceded in my behalf was dressed like the others in a yellow feather cape and crested helmet. But he carried the largest torch, and wore around his neck an ivory whale-tooth hook and a black image of the ancient god, Lono."

Penni Pulianano! Somehow Vicki held back the words. Instead she asked, "And they agreed? The three marchers agreed to spare you?" Vicki asked the question as if she believed every bit of Lili's tale.

"They agreed on one condition," Lili said. "I had to promise to move to Hale Maile before the full moon and never again visit Reef Royal or walk in the jungle after that time."

"A strange request, don't you think?" Vicki asked.

"The warriors said that my near presence disturbed their marches and that if I wished to live I would obey their command. That's why I'm moving, but I certainly can't tell your aunt such a tale; the whole city of Honolulu would think I had gone crazy. Sometimes I even doubt my own sanity. I've continued to take my walks each evening, and I plan to continue them until the deadline for my moving in the hope that perhaps the marchers will return and revoke my sentence."

"Lili, I think someone is trying to scare you away from Reef Royal, some enemy of

147

Aunt Noel's. I think this whole night marcher bit is nothing but a hoax." Vicki glanced at her watch. It was almost dinner time and she needed a few moments to think all these strange things through and to sort them out in her mind before she said any more to anyone.

"I must go now, Lili," Vicki said. "Forgive me for prying into your affairs, but I hope I can do something to persuade you to remain at Reef Royal. Please think over what I've just said to you."

"It is too late," Lili whispered. "The marchers were real, Vicki. They command; I obey."

Chapter Eleven

Although it was dinner time and she knew her aunt would be waiting for her, Vicki ducked into her own room. She needed to be alone, to sort her confused thoughts. Her mind raced back to the time only a few short hours ago when she had believed that learning Lili's reason for moving would solve all problems for the Foster family. Was life always like this? Was it a rule of nature that the answer to one puzzle would merely form a bright link in a long chain of more urgent questions?

Vicki could hardly believe that an intelligent woman like Lili would believe a silly superstition, yet simple arithmetic told her that Lili was a child during days when Hawaii was still part Christian and part pagan. And she knew that the human memory was an intaglio of childhood impressions, highly emotional impressions that defied reason.

But Night Marchers! What a hoax! Vicki wanted to run to her aunt's room to tell the whole family why Lili planned to move, then to relax while Aunt Noel talked Lili out of such silly notions. Yet she knew this wouldn't work. In the first place she had promised Lili not to tell anyone who would laugh, and such a story revealed to a group would certainly bring smiles. Then, after the smiles, the family was sure to consider the same questions Vicki had asked herself. Perhaps after she had some of the answers she would be able to discuss the matter privately with her aunt.

Vicki sighed. She knew she was only postponing the inevitable. Someone was playing a cruel trick on Lili, and she didn't have to think twice to figure out who it was. Lili's descriptive story of the Night Marchers left little doubt in Vicki's mind that Penni Pulianano was deeply involved in the fraud.

First, the golden cape tied in with Penni's yellow-stained fingers. Vicki knew from her reading that the feather capes of the ancient royalty were valuable museum pieces. If Lili saw such a cape, it must have been a rented costume or, more likely, one made especially for the occasion — perhaps with a fringe of home-dyed chicken feathers to give it the illusion of authenticity.

Then there was the burn on Penni's hand — the injury he tried to hide and refused to discuss. Even a person accustomed to carrying a torch might suffer an accidental burn if he were under great stress and became careless and excited. But this was merely speculation.

The factor which made Vicki positive that Penni was involved in Lili's troubles was her description of the pendants which the leader of the Night Marchers wore around his neck. It was highly unlikely that two people would be wearing both an ivory whale's tooth and a black-carved image of Lono. Vicki was convinced. Penni was the culprit. But now came the real stickler. Why? Why would it be to his advantage to frighten Lili? Did he have some personal reason for wanting her to abandon Reef Royal? And if so, what was it? Why would a beach boy be interested in Lili Lanuoka?

"Vicki, we're waiting dinner on you." Buzz called outside her door.

"Coming, Buzz." Vicki washed her hands and ran a cooling cloth over her face before joining the family at her aunt's table. As she sat down, she thought that her cousins looked at her strangely, yet she knew they couldn't possibly see the thoughts that choked the surface of her mind like a tangle of seaweed. Vicki ate her meal without quite knowing how it tasted. Buzz commented on

151

the delicious rice, and she found herself nodding in agreement although she much preferred mashed potatoes.

"Holly tells me that you plan to enter Lili's writing contest," Aunt Noel said. "How are you coming along?"

"I'll soon have my story ready to submit," Vicki answered. "Everyone I talk to thinks that Holly will win this year, but at least I'll have the fun of having something entered." Vicki tried to sound carefree, tried to make her relatives believe that her interest in writing was a casual thing. Only to herself would she admit the truth.

Mark joined the conversation about the writing competition, and Vicki thought that he seemed a little more friendly toward her now that he knew she planned to enter the contest. But she could never tell about Mark. His manner might be put on for his mother's benefit. Vicki couldn't quite believe that Mark's attitude toward her had changed even when he went so far as to walk to the dining room with her after they finished eating. She was afraid that he was going to quiz her about her second date with Penni, and she was relieved as well as surprised when he ignored that subject.

"Vicki," Mark said, "I know you had good intentions when you questioned Mrs.

Wong about Lili, and I'm sorry I was so rude to you."

"That's all right, Mark." Vicki wished she could confide her secret about the Night Marchers to her cousin, but she didn't dare to do that just yet. Perhaps his good mood was only a fleeting thing; perhaps if she voiced her suspicions about Penni, Mark would retreat into his shell of hostility and retort, "I-told-you-so." She decided to keep her suspicions to herself a bit longer; telling Mark would do absolutely no good. If he lost his temper, it might do a great deal of harm.

Vicki went straight to her room as soon as she finished her evening duties. She flopped across her bed, closed her eyes, and forced herself to review every minute of the time she'd spent with Penni Pulianano. It was a slow and painful process, but at last her memories and her suppositions began to dovetail. She jumped to her feet.

Lafe Yankton! Why had she been so slow to catch on? Lafe Yankton was the person who would profit most from Lili's change of residence — Lafe Yankton, who had given Penni cash upon demand.

Vicki recalled Penni's saying that in a few days he would have money for a car of his own. That was it. This rival hotel man must have hired Penni and some pals to masquerade as Night Marchers with the agreement that he would get his pay only if he were successful in persuading Lili to move. The ten dollars he had given Penni last night must have been an advance, a mere part of the total sum.

Bits and pieces of ideas and conversations began to form a scrappy picture in Vicki's mind, and she knew now what she had to do. She had to act quickly before she lost her nerve. If her idea worked, it would more than make up to Aunt Noel and Mark for the trouble and embarrassment she had caused by questioning Mrs. Wong, and it would also enable her to keep Lili's secret in good faith.

Without bothering to change from her working clothes, Vicki hurried from her room, cut across the moonlit lawn and parking area, then crossed the wide asphalt street in front of Hale Maile.

Stepping inside the border of tall Norfolk pines that guarded the hotel grounds like a belt of dark spikes, Vicki paused and looked around. She heard voices murmuring from the hotel lobby, and then near a flickering patio torch she saw Lafe Yankton sitting in a lawn chair like a fat, albino toad waiting for its unsuspecting prey. From somewhere the wind picked up the nauseating stench of rotting coral, and Vicki felt her stomach contract into a hard knot as she forced herself to walk calmly to the spot where Lafe sat.

"What do you want?" Lafe's voice grated like sand against glass.

"I'm Vicki Foster." Vicki fought to keep her tone steady.

"I know who you are," Lafe said. "What do you want at Hale Maile?"

Vicki hesitated for a moment. She had expected Lafe Yankton to be curious, but his abrupt manner frightened her. Taking a deep breath, she swallowed a wedge that suddenly blocked her throat. It was too late to retreat.

"Why are you trying to frighten Lili Lanuoka away from my aunt's hotel?" Vicki blurted out.

If Lafe Yankton was surprised at her pointed question he failed to show it. "Lili Lanuoka comes to Hale Maile of her own accord. If your aunt has sent you here to make trouble, she's out of line. If Lili says she'll move, there's no way to stop her."

"You've tricked her." Vicki was surprised at her ability to stand up to this man who wasn't reacting in the least as she had thought he would. "I know that you hired Penni Pulianano and his friends to mas-

155

querade as Marchers in the Night and to frighten Lili into obeying your wishes. You deliberately took advantage of her Hawaiian background and her trusting nature."

"You have proof of all this, I suppose?" Lafe taunted.

"I have all the proof I need." Vicki spoke with unaccustomed assurance.

Lafe Yankton gave a superior laugh. "Why has your aunt sent *you* here? Is she afraid to face me in person?"

"Aunt Noel has no idea that I'm here," Vicki said. "Nor has Lili. But if you won't promise me to drop your grubby scheme against Reef Royal, I intend to go straight to my aunt and tell her the whole story. I've only kept it a secret this long to protect Lili's feelings."

Lafe snorted. "You expect me to believe that! I know Noelani Foster. She's done her best to put me out of business. You tell her that if she thinks she can scare me by sending you over here with a silly threat . . ." Lafe's voice died to a mere throaty gurgle.

"But Aunt Noel didn't send me," Vicki insisted.

Lafe's eyes bulged in his pasty face as he made an agonized effort to rise to his feet, and although Vicki still towered several inches above him, she instinctively took a step backward.

"I can have you arrested for threatening me, Miss Foster. And if your aunt wants a game of name calling and mud slinging, I can qualify as a prime participant. You'd better believe me and you'd better leave these premises before you start some real trouble."

Vicki's courage suddenly evaporated like a mist from the valley and she hurried half-sobbing back toward Reef Royal. Her visit to Hale Maile seemed like a crazy nightmare. How could her idea have failed so miserably? Had all her theories been wrong? Vicki doubted that they had, yet could Lafe Yankton dare threaten her with arrest unless he were innocent of her charges?

Vicki ran through the Reef Royal lobby, passed Mark without speaking, bumped into Buzz, and only slowed momentarily as she almost knocked into an elderly guest who was studying the bulletin board. When she reached her room she was still trying to figure out what she must do next. Again her best intentions had only made matters worse for the Fosters. She should have known that a man daring enough to form a plan like masquerading night spirits wouldn't let a girl stand in his way to success.

What would Aunt Noel think if Lafe Yankton caused a public scandal by calling the police? And what would the family do if he spread ugly rumors about Reef Royal? Vicki knew that the hotel would lose business when Lili moved. This blow in addition to Lafe Yankton's smear tactics could mean the end of the Fosters' business.

Chapter Twelve

A soft tapping on her door brought Vicki to attention as suddenly as if someone had blown a police whistle. Had Lafe Yankton already stormed to Reef Royal to make trouble? Vicki wished she had an ally, someone to stand up for her and to protect her. She opened the door and smiled weakly as she saw only Aunt Noel standing there.

"Vicki! Whatever is the matter? Are you sick?"

"No, Aunt Noel, I'm fine, but I'm tired. I was just getting ready for bed."

Aunt Noel stepped into the room. "I'll only keep you a moment, Vicki. I've been talking to Lili. She plans to visit her aunt on the valley island of Maui tomorrow, and she wants you to accompany her. You're due for a day off from hotel duty, you know. Please go. It'll be an interesting trip for you, and Lili needs a traveling companion to help with flight schedules and cabs. Ever since the inter-island passenger-boat service was discontinued Lili has been reluctant to leave Oahu."

"I'd love to go with her," Vicki said. "But won't we need reservations ahead of time?" Her mind was like a dragging anchor trying to halt this forward motion into tomorrow. How could Lili think of taking a trip at a time like this!

"Mark's calling the airport now," Aunt Noel answered. "And don't worry about expenses; Lili has two unexpiring passes on Aloha Airlines. Why don't you go around to her apartment and learn the details of the trip. And Vicki. I should tell you that you're receiving a high honor. Lili only asks those of whom she is genuinely fond to visit this ancient relative with her."

Vicki thanked her aunt, then went to Lili's apartment. As she knocked on the door, it opened so quickly that Vicki knew Lili must have been listening for her step in the hallway.

The inside of the apartment surprised Vicki. She hardly recognized it as the same place she'd visited in the daytime. Soft, indirect lighting accentuated the ancient Hawaiian aspects of Lili's life, and all indications of modern America were minimized in the dimness. Vicki felt as if she had stepped into another age as she inhaled the mingled odors of sandalwood and plumeria.

"I hope you've come to say you'll fly to Maui with me tomorrow, Vicki."

Vicki couldn't be rude, much as she hated the idea of leaving Oahu. "I'd love to go, Lili." Vicki knew her face must be a map of curiosity, because Lili began answering her questions before she asked them.

"I love to visit the outer islands, Vicki, but this is more than a pleasure trip. I've been considering your thought that some persons played a cruel trick on me by masquerading as Night Marchers. This is possible, but I must learn the truth. Can you understand how I feel, Vicki? Years ago I decided to follow Christian teachings, although it was difficult for me to give up the old Hawaiian way of life. I suppose everyone doubts the wisdom of his decisions at times. But I haven't felt so confused since I was a child."

"How will a trip to Maui help?" Vicki asked.

"My mother's sister lives in the mountains of Maui. Aunt Naniloa is an old, old lady now, but her mind is still sharp. Her father-in-law once saw the Marchers and lived to speak of it. I'll tell her exactly what happened to me in the jungle, and she'll know from hearing of his experience whether or not I am the victim of a hoax."

Vicki frowned. "But can your Aunt Naniloa remember verifying details after so many years?"

"Such memories are etched permanently in the minds of Hawaiians."

Lili's statement was final, and Vicki knew it was useless to argue. Perhaps this was a wise move. Maybe this old aunt would point out some flaw in Lili's experience — some inconsistency that would convince her that Lili had been tricked. Maybe, Vicki thought, she could depend on Aunt Naniloa for the support she herself sought and needed.

"I'll be ready, Lili. What time is our flight?"

"We must be at the airport by seven-thirty. We'll spend most of the day on Maui and return to Oahu in the afternoon. Get a good night's sleep, Vicki, and I'll see you in the morning."

Vicki had so many things on her mind that she knew she wouldn't sleep a wink. What if Lafe Yankton kept his threat to cause trouble while she was away? What would the family do when they learned that she had meddled again — this time dangerously — in their affairs? Vicki closed her eyes and thought about the future — about that pleasant carefree time when she and Greg would be married. Finally, in spite of her troubles, regrets, worries, Vicki fell asleep and didn't waken until her alarm jangled the next morning.

The hurry-scurry of preparing for a trip kept Vicki's mind from serious matters, and before she knew it, Mark was escorting Lili to the car for the ride to the airport, and Buzz was decorating them both with leis.

"These are Globe Amaranth," he said before Vicki could ask. "Since you fuss so about wilting flowers, I decided to give you a lei that will last forever."

"Forever?" Vicki asked.

"Well, almost." Buzz laughed. "You can let these blossoms dry and they'll keep their purple color indefinitely."

Vicki smiled and waved her thanks as Mark impolitely drove off.

The airport whirled in general hub-bub like a carnival midway despite the early hour. Mark checked their reservations and found them seats near their departure gate before saying good-bye and disappearing into the crowd.

Vicki brooded silently during the twenty minutes before they were allowed to board the red, white, and blue Aloha jet, but once they found their seats she thought only of the exciting day ahead.

Lili suggested that Vicki take the window seat as she herself became giddy whenever she looked down or out at such a great height. They both fastened their seat belts for takeoff, and as the smell of diesel exhaust overpowered the fragrance of the many leis in the plane, Vicki felt the engine vibration shake the floorboards. They taxied down the runway with propeller whine blotting out all other sound. Vicki relaxed. They were airborne.

The large oval window was like an enchanted looking glass. Peering through it Vicki felt a chill prickle the base of her neck as she watched the earth fall away. The inlets of Pearl Harbor looked like blue, stubby fingers, and the National Cemetery in Punchbowl Crater was a contrasting study in green and white. Dark clouds threatened the distant mountains, but they were far away. Vicki stared out and down until Diamond Head and Koko Head craters were behind them and they were over the ocean.

The dark-haired stewardess barely had time to give safety instructions, to serve glasses of hot, steaming coffee, and to point out the Dole pineapple fields on the island of Lanai on their right and the palm-fringed harbor of Molokai on their left before Vicki felt the plane lose altitude in preparation for landing. The touchdown was smooth, and it was only when they braked to a sharp stop that Vicki noticed that Lili had been sitting with her eyes tightly closed.

"We've landed, Lili." By the time Vicki had unfastened her seat belt, the stewardess had arrived to help Lili whose ample proportions all but overflowed the small airline seats. When they were finally off the plane and walking on firm Maui ground, Lili relaxed, and Vicki realized that their flight had been anything but pleasurable for the old Hawaiian lady.

"How often do you visit your aunt?" Vicki asked.

"I try to get here twice a year," Lili answered. "Sue used to make the trip with me. Sometimes she would rent a car and deliver me to Aunt Naniloa's home, then drive on to Lahaina, the old whaling capital of the islands, to spend the day. But you'd better plan to stay with me. I want you to meet Aunt Naniloa and to hear what she has to say."

Vicki found Lili a seat inside the terminal building and went to arrange for transportation to Aunt Naniloa's home. When she explained that she was Lili's companion, the cab driver beamed and hurried over to greet Lili. It was obvious that she was a known and welcome guest on Maui, and many times during their drive along the eucalyptus-lined road the driver smiled at Vicki and helped Lili point out to her the soft-green cane fields, the darker blue-green pineapple beds, and a wide variety of orchids, anthurium, and ginger.

"Does your aunt ever visit you in Honolulu?" Vicki asked as they drove higher into the mountains.

"Never." Lili sighed. "And you'll be appalled at her hut. I've tried, begged, and pleaded to get her to move, to come live with me, but Maui is her home. She's convinced that she owes her long life to the eucalyptus trees here on Maui which absorb much harmful moisture from the air. What a stubborn one! Nobody can change her mind."

Driving by fenced fields and pastures where giant green cactus grew like twisted refugees from some long-remembered desert, Vicki watched sleek, grazing cattle. Then, as their car reached higher altitudes on the mountain road, clouds masked the sun, and Vicki felt cooler air fan her cheeks as she inhaled the clean smell of rain.

Their driver turned onto a winding red-dirt path and shifted gears for another steep climb, but Lili stopped him.

"This is far enough, thank you. We'll walk the last few steps to the house. Please return for us in three hours."

Vicki felt abandoned when the cab disappeared from sight, and Lili leaned heavily on her arm as they plodded up the dusty, brick-red lane to a weathered, unkempt shack that stood like a moulting gull in a pine-rimmed clearing.

Before they could rap on the door it creaked open, and a woman much larger than Lili stood squeezed into the entryway. The leathery brown skin of her face hung in drooping, wrinkled folds, the thinness of her gray hair bespoke great age, but her eyes were sharp, bright, and inquisitive as a puppy's.

"Lili!" the woman cried. "Aloha! Aloha! It is a good omen when you come to visit your old aunt." Then as if she had noticed Vicki for the first time, she said, "And who is this *haole wahine?*"

Vicki felt ill at ease. She'd read enough from a Hawaiian phrase book to know that Aunt Naniloa had referred to her as a "white girl," and somehow the title seemed ominous.

"Aunt Naniloa, I want you to meet Vicki Foster. She's Sue's cousin from the mainland."

Vicki held out her hand, but the old aunt merely nodded and stepped back so they could enter her home. She dragged up two straight-backed bamboo chairs for them, then sank down onto a wide rattan rocker that was obviously where she spent much time.

As she looked around, Vicki inhaled a pleasant spicy odor rising from a kettle that simmered gently on the back of an old wood stove. The pandanus floor matting was clean but badly worn, and Vicki heard their chairs creak at the joints. But on the center of a carved table was an artfully arranged bouquet of wood roses and bird-of-paradise blossoms displayed in the hollowed-out half of a yellow calabash. Vicki had to admit that the hut had charm in spite of its neglected appearance.

Lili and her aunt exchanged a few pleasantries, then Lili spoke of the reason for her visit. She told her aunt of her experience with the Marchers in the Night, described them in minute detail, and asked the older woman's opinion on the matter.

"Oh, Lili! Lili! You have no choice. If you want to live you must obey the marchers,"

Aunt Naniloa replied. "Only last week they murdered Akoha Pelento. It was sad — sad."

"But how do you know that Night Marchers were responsible?" Vicki joined the conversation for the first time.

"Akoha's neighbors found him lying dead mid-way on the mountain trail leading to his home." Aunt Naniloa spoke as if certain facts were not to be questioned.

Vicki said nothing, but she thought that if this unfortunate Hawaiian had been as fat as Aunt Naniloa, it was quite possible that he had died of natural causes — a heart attack or a stroke of apoplexy.

"Vicki thought that the marchers might be a hoax, that someone might be trying to trick me into leaving Reef Royal," Lili said at last.

"Vicki!" Aunt Naniloa spat the word as if to hold it longer would dirty her mouth. "Lili, *I,* I your Aunt Naniloa, your aunt who was once advisor to kings, have spoken the truth about the Marchers in the Night. Who is this Vicki? Indeed! Why do you even listen to her *haole* theories?"

Aunt Naniloa struggled to her feet, her dark eyes snapping and her face flushing purple with strain and anger. "First the thieving missionaries come and steal the very islands from under Hawaiian feet, and now you sit there, Lili Lanuoka, you sit there willing to listen to words that will snuff out your life. If the Marchers say move, you must pack and go. This *haole wahine* is plotting against you."

Vicki stood up, angry and embarrassed, but Lili spoke in a rather tired, sad tone.

"I respect your wisdom and knowledge of the past, Aunt Naniloa, but you are unwittingly nourishing grudges you must have inherited from your royal parents. The missionaries came to the islands to help us, and to show us the foolishness of our pagan ways. After all these years, can you not understand that?"

Aunt Naniloa thrashed about the room like an enraged shark trapped in shallow water. "The missionaries loved the islands, but they despised the Hawaiians, Lili. They let our people die by the thousands. The missionaries watched and did nothing while a trusting race put its foot on the rainbow to oblivion."

"Aunt! Aunt! It was the missionaries who made the islands prosper. They gave us much — the cane, the pineapple, but their most important gift was their sons and daughters. These educated families saved Hawaii from degeneration."

"Please, ladies." Vicki saw the old aunt shaking with emotion. "Forgive me for starting such an argument. Lili, I have upset your aunt and you needn't defend me. While you finish your visit, I'll wait outside."

Vicki hurried from the house and ran back down the red dusty path to the main road. No wonder Sue rented a car and spent the day in Lahaina when she visited Maui! Aunt Naniloa was crotchety and unreasonable. Vicki flopped down on the grass beneath a hau tree and blinked back tears of frustration. She appreciated Lili's trying to defend her, and she was truly sorry their visit had upset Aunt Naniloa, but she was even more sorry to think that in spite of her modern education Lili would probably base an overriding decision on her aunt's mistaken, superstitious ideas.

Chapter Thirteen

As Vicki sat in the shade of the hau tree sorting her ruffled feelings, she realized that she was more disappointed than angry — disappointed because Aunt Naniloa had found no flaws in Lili's story and had assured her that she must obey the Marchers' command. Vicki was embarrassed to have caused such a bitter family argument, but she couldn't blame Aunt Naniloa for her cutting words. She pitied the aging *alii*, who was still trying to live in a world that had disappeared decades ago.

Feeling very much alone, Vicki stood, strolled to the edge of the mountain road, and looked out across the narrow valley below. On her far right and her far left the undulating ocean hugged the ribbons of white sand beach that trimmed the green cane fields, and directly across the valley more mountains stood like imposing monarchs guarding their palace grounds. Just as she settled back down under the hau tree for a long wait, she heard a door close and saw Lili walking down the path.

"I'm sorry, Vicki," Lili said. "I had no idea that our visit would upset Aunt Naniloa so. I'd forgotten about her distrust of white people as well as her resentment of Hawaiian statehood. I'm afraid your presence galled her memory."

"But is she right about her accusations?" Vicki asked. "It's awful to think of the Hawaiian race dying. It's so — so final."

Lili eased down beside Vicki in the soft grass. "Yes, it's happening, Vicki. But Aunt Naniloa blames the wrong people. The old Hawaiians had little resistance to the diseases that the whaling ships brought to the islands. A sailor's simple case of measles meant wide-spread death when the Hawaiians caught the germ. Had the plantation owners not brought in Chinese and Japanese to work in the cane fields, the Hawaiians would have died off completely. These missionary descendants saved our race in many ways."

"You mean that intermarriage with disease-resistant Orientals saved the Hawaiians?"

Lili nodded. "There are only a handful of pureblood Hawaiians in all the islands today. But, come, we can't solve the problems of Hawaii here on this mountainside." She struggled to her feet. "We'll catch an early flight back to Honolulu, then I must finish packing. Aunt Naniloa may be confused about modern times, but I respect her opinions concerning our old native beliefs.'"

Ignoring the latter part of Lili's statement, Vicki asked, "But how can we catch an early flight? Our cab won't return for hours."

"We'll start walking. Perhaps someone will offer us a ride."

"Lili! No hitch-hiking! And it's too far to walk. Why we're miles and miles from that airport." In all the time Vicki had been waiting under the hau tree, no car had passed along the road. This hushed, rural section of Maui was nothing like the noisy, bustling hub-bub of Honolulu.

"Come." Like a dignified judge Lili overruled Vicki's objection.

As they sauntered down the road, Vicki heard the whir of tires against black-top and turned to see a battered truck heaped with pineapple approaching. As the vehicle stopped, a sweet, cloying fragrance stifled them, and the driver leaned his dark head out the window to ask if they wanted a ride.

To Vicki's relief Lili shook her head, thanked the man, and continued walking. When the truck disappeared around a bend in the road she said, "We can do better than that."

They walked many minutes in silence before another car approached. Lili took one look at it, and to Vicki's chagrin she stepped forward to flag it down. "Don't worry, child. It's a touring car. If it's not filled, the driver will welcome two extra fares."

Lili was right. There were empty seats in the twelve-passenger limousine, and the driver as well as the tourists welcomed them after Lili explained their situation.

Motoring through the lush cane fields, the tour guide suddenly braked the car as billows of black-sweet-smelling smoke blocked his vision.

"What's happened, Lili?" Vicki asked. "Is the cane field afire?" Her eyes watered and she choked as pungent smoke swirled through the car before they could close the windows. What else could possibly happen on this ill-fated trip!

To Vicki's surprise their driver was smiling as he inched them through the smoke-laden area. His voice droned reassuringly over the car microphone as he explained that the cane fields were burned intentionally to facilitate the harvest.

Ignoring the burnt-sugar taste in her mouth, Vicki peered into the smoke-shrouded fields until she made out wide fire breaks and saw plantation hands controlling the blaze. As they emerged from the smoky area, they passed one black-charred field that had already been burned free of useless leaves. Only the cane stalks heavy with syrup remained standing.

Vicki was glad when they left the cane fields behind, and was more than pleased when they reached the airport where the tourists waved them friendly farewells as they left the limousine.

Luckily, they had only a short wait before their jet flight back to Oahu, and when they arrived at the Honolulu airport, Vicki left Lili in the waiting room while she phoned Reef Royal for transportation.

Mark came to meet them, and although he was surprised at their early arrival, he asked few questions. During their silent ride through the city Vicki reached a decision. She would take Mark into her confidence. She had promised Lili to reveal her experience to no one who would laugh, and telling Mark wouldn't break her promise. Vicki couldn't imagine Mark really laughing at anything.

Mark let them out in front of the hotel, and while he drove to the parking area, Vicki accompanied Lili to her apartment, thanked her for the trip, then rushed to find her cousin before she lost her nerve.

"Mark!" Vicki met him as he walked across the back *lanai*. "Mark, where can we talk?"

"Anywhere, I suppose." Mark shrugged his shoulders as if she bored him.

"I mean where can we talk in *private?*"

Mark sighed. "Well, if you've got problems, come on down to Mother's rooms. She's at the lobby desk; we'll be alone."

Vicki followed Mark to Aunt Noel's rooms and when he closed the door behind them she blurted out her story. She revealed Lili's fear of Night Marchers, her own suspicions of Penni Pulianano, and also her rash visit to Lafe Yankton.

"You were right about Penni, Mark. I would have been smart to avoid a second date with him."

"So now you know." Mark's words were cold.

"Lafe Yankton hasn't — hasn't *done* anything yet, has he?" Vicki's mouth went dry as she asked the question.

"No, we've seen or heard nothing of him." Mark paced silently back and forth across the room, and Vicki felt as if she were waiting for a volcano to erupt. But when at last he spoke his voice was calm as early morning.

"Your story isn't too hard to believe,

Vicki; I wouldn't put such a trick past Penni. It's Lili's falling for the scheme that gets me."

"Try to understand her, Mark," Vicki said. "Try to imagine what it must have been like."

"What *what* must have been like?"

"A childhood in the days of the monarchy," Vicki said. "Lili has much dignity and wisdom, but can't you imagine how terribly hard it must have been for her to discard the teachings and ideas of her parents and to replace them with the more modern ideas brought here by the missionaries. I can certainly understand how she can still have some blind spots."

"Well, I suppose Aunt Naniloa did nothing to straighten out Lili's thinking," Mark said.

"Right. And the old aunt was so bad tempered that I'm surprised that Lili ever goes to Maui."

"Don't judge Maui by one person," Mark said. "I worked over there for a few weeks when I was in college. It's a lovely place."

"Mark, I have an idea." Vicki saw a cautious look close Mark's face like a shade drawn across an open window. She couldn't blame him for being wary.

"You've had several ideas already, it

seems to me." He gave a grunt. "But I have none of my own, so let's hear yours."

"Since I've no proof to back up my suspicions we'll have to catch Penni in the act of masquerading as a Night Marcher and make him personally admit his hoax to Lili."

"Simple! Simple!" Mark straddled a chair, resting his arms across the back as he stared at his cousin. "Tell me more."

"You'll have to help," Vicki said.

"I figured as much." Mark frowned. "And what have you planned for me?"

"Mark, this is serious." Vicki stood up as if her very height might make her plan seem more worthy. "I'll disguise myself as Lili and follow her usual pattern of walking in the evening. Then, when the marchers appear, you'll tackle Penni and make him confess."

"Pardon me, cousin, but there are a few holes in this scheme of yours." Mark rose, and as he looked down at Vicki, she suddenly felt that he saw through her impulsive scheme — saw the doubt that filled her.

"Number one." Like a school teacher Mark wagged his forefinger at her. "How do you know the marchers will appear again? Number two, what's Lili going to think when she sees you walking her usual rounds? Number three . . ."

"Wait, Mark." Vicki was determined to

stand up for her plan. Good or bad, it was their only hope. She had to believe in it — to make the most of it. "One thing at a time. We can force the Marchers to appear again if we make Penni believe that Lili's changed her mind about moving. I have a hunch that Penni's new car depends a lot on the payment he hopes to receive from Lafe Yankton, and I have a feeling he'll do anything, anything at all to keep his end of their bargain."

"So you call Penni on the phone and tell him to get in costume and forward march." Mark snorted. "It'll never do, Vicki."

"It has to work, Mark. It's our only chance to keep Lili here. Where's Buzz? He can help."

"It's a crazy idea," Mark said, "and we have nothing much to lose, but do we have to drag Buzz into this? He only has two speeds, slow and stop. What can he do that we can't do more quickly ourselves?"

"There he goes." Vicki pointed to Buzz who was sauntering across the lawn. Then before Mark could stop her, she stepped to the *lanai* and called to him.

"What's up?" Buzz asked, seeing their serious expressions.

Vicki repeated her story while Mark shook his head in discouragement and Buzz listened in disbelief. "Buzz, you *have* to help us. You know Penni. He'd think nothing of it if you were to visit with him about that surfboard you're buying. Using that as an opening, you could casually mention that Lili has decided to remain at Reef Royal. If my theory's correct, Penni'll stage another march in a final attempt to secure payment from Lafe."

"I can't do it, Vicki," Buzz said. "When I tell fibs my ears turn pink and give me away."

"Oh, for Pete's sake, Buzz," Mark said. "Be serious! You won't be telling a fib. If our plan works out, Lili won't be moving; you'll just be telling a premature truth."

Vicki felt hope surge within her like a tidal wave as she heard Mark speak of "our plan," and she went on to explain her second idea.

"Buzz, another thing, you'll have to keep Lili from taking her walk tomorrow night. As Mark pointed out, we can't have two Lili's strolling about at the same time."

"Tomorrow night!" Buzz said. "And how am I going to stop her?"

"It has to be tomorrow," Vicki said. "It's too late to organize this plan today. There's no way we can delay the end of the writing contest, but we have to spring this trap on Penni tomorrow night, Sunday. Lili plans to move out Monday morning. How you'll stop her from taking her walk will be strictly up to you, Buzz. Maybe you can think of some other way for her to get her daily exercise. But I know you'll come up with something. I'll filch one of Lili's full-cut, ankle-length muumuus from the laundry room and also one of Sue's floppy straw hats. I'm almost as tall as Lili, and in the dusk with a few pillows for padding and with my hair covered by a hat, I'll look like a true *alii* — I hope."

"What if Penni senses a trap and cuts out?" Buzz asked.

"We have to make sure that doesn't happen," Vicki said. "If Mark tackles Penni, it's a good bet that the other two impostors will be so surprised and frightened that they'll run — especially if you and I make a lot of noise, Buzz, make them think we have a militia on our side. Oh, and one more thing, Buzz. Bring your camera along and snap a flash of Penni — a shot that he can't deny and that we can use for evidence if necessary."

"Gee, Vicki, you've thought of everything," Buzz said.

"Everything and then some." Mark's words were sarcastic, but Vicki heard the lilt of hope in his voice and knew that he would do his best to make her ideas work out for them. For the first time since she arrived at Reef Royal Vicki felt that she and Mark were at least working toward the same goal. It was good to have someone helping her — to have an ally.

Chapter Fourteen

Vicki still had the rest of the day off, but she wished she didn't; she needed some work to occupy her mind as well as her hands. Now that their plans for the following evening were set, she wanted to forget them until then. The whole scheme seemed like a game of make-believe being played by fictitious characters on an imaginary island.

Vicki pleaded exhaustion to her aunt and asked to be excused from dinner. After eating a sandwich in her room, she settled down at the desk to tackle the drawings she had decided would enhance her story. Although Mark was convinced that Holly would win the scholarship, Vicki remembered Lili's pleased smile as she read sketches from Vicki's journal. Lili wouldn't praise mediocre work and Lili had urged her to enter the contest. Thus encouraged, Vicki felt that she had a chance to win if she submitted her story before the midnight deadline. Perhaps there wouldn't be too many children's tales, and even if she missed the grand prize, it would be rewarding to see something she had written in print in Lili's anthology. But enough dreaming. Gripping a charcoal stick she hunched over her paper and began a trial sketch of a giraffe.

Hours later when a few good sketches covered her desk, and many discarded ones littered the floor, Vicki stood up and stretched her aching muscles. But before she had time to assemble the drawings with the story pages, someone knocked on her door.

"Vicki," Mark called. "Telegram in the lobby!"

Vicki opened the door, thanked Mark, and hurried down the hallway to the hotel desk where a blue-uniformed messenger waited.

"Sign here, Miss," he said.

Vicki eyed the yellow envelope, and her charcoal-blackened fingers perspired as she signed the register. Was it good news? Bad news? An emergency? Never before had she received a telegram.

As the messenger left the hotel, Vicki dropped onto a bamboo couch and ripped open the envelope. She scanned the message quickly and felt her heart pound like a kettledrum as she went back to reread it slowly.

"Dear Vicki Stop I love you Stop Let's be married soon Stop We need each other and we're foolish not to admit it Stop I'll carry minimum college hours and work part time so that we can be together Stop all my love Stop

Greg"

Vicki was dazzled, yet at the same time she felt as if someone had pulled a rug from under her feet. So Greg wanted them to be married! He had their life all planned; all she had to do was to agree.

But it wasn't that easy. Vicki slipped the telegram back into its envelope and sat with her eyes closed, thinking. Greg's message scotched her theory that a girl could always anticipate a proposal. Or did it? She remembered that last letter she'd written to Greg, the one after her frightening experience with Penni, the one in which she'd admitted how lonesome, worried, and troubled she was. She sighed as she realized that one small letter impulsively written in a moment of despair had destroyed the result of all her careful plans for their last date in San Francisco. Yet she wasn't entirely sorry. Greg's proposal thrilled her. Marriage was the dream she yearned for. Maybe she could get a job, too, even without business training.

"Oh, there you are, Vicki." Lili's voice whipped across the lobby like a lasso to jerk her back to reality. "I'll be disappointed if you don't turn in a contest entry. The deadline is near."

Vicki opened her eyes and tried to focus her thoughts on Lili's words. "I'll get it to you before midnight," she said. "I only have to assemble the pages."

"Vicki, what's the matter?" Lili scrutinized her face. "Your cheeks are flushed and your eyes are watery. Are you ill, child?"

Vicki could sense Mark overhearing their conversation from his post at the lobby desk, but she didn't care. "I'm fine, Lili." Vicki fingered the envelope in her lap and laughed nervously. "I just received a wire from Greg, my boyfriend on the mainland. He wants us to be married soon." She blurted out the words, although a minute earlier she'd intended to keep the proposal a secret.

"And do you plan to accept?" Lili sat down beside her.

"I'm not sure." Lili's question galvanized her decision. "But I rather think I will."

"What about college?" Lili asked. "It's none of my business, but it seems to me that a girl should get all the education she can before she marries. And you are interested in writing. I know you are."

187

"I can learn to write after we are married." Vicki sighed. "Greg and I are in love. How much better for me to be married, to find a job, and to help Greg finish school than for me to waste four years in college." Vicki smiled at Lili, waiting for her approval, but to her surprise Lili's eyes lost their childlike sparkle and she frowned and shook her head.

"You disappoint me, Vicki. I suspect that you're afraid! You're afraid to try life on your own, and you're using Greg and marriage to bolster your self-confidence. You want to slide gently from the security of your parents' home to the safety of a home with Greg without ever risking standing on your own two feet."

"That's unfair, Lili!" Vicki's voice was knife-sharp as she replied to Lili's unusually blunt words, but she didn't care.

"Perhaps you're right," Lili said, "but why do you consider marriage the only alternative for those who don't go to college? Why not set some other goal for yourself, then do your best to achieve it? You're full of ideas, Vicki, and an idea can take a person a long way." Lili settled herself more comfortably on the couch, and Vicki braced herself to listen to an unwelcome lecture, all the while wishing for escape.

"Try life on your own, Vicki. Don't rush into marriage."

"How old were you when you married, Lili?" Vicki asked.

"I was sixteen," Lili said. "And my parents chose my husband for me."

"You seem to have survived the whole affair very nicely." Vicki's voice was triumphant. "You're rich, famous, and still working actively, although you're far past retirement age."

"You disappoint me, Vicki." Lili said no more. She stood and walked toward her apartment, and Vicki felt ashamed of herself for pinning Lili down as to her age at marriage and thus quashing all her arguments.

I'll apologize when I take my story to her, Vicki thought. She rose to go to her room, smiled at Mark at the lobby desk, and wondered how much of their conversation he'd heard.

Back at her desk Vicki tried to forget Lili Lanuoka's advice, but the old lady's gritty words stuck to her mind like sand on wet skin. She'd dated few boys before she started going steady with Greg, and although she hated to admit it, she knew that her inexperience was the very thing that had kept her from realizing sooner what a wild, uncouth boy Penni Pulianano was.

But Lili had mentioned ideas. Were ideas such an asset? All through school Vicki's friends had teased her about her crazy plans and unusual schemes. Ideas — some good, some bad. It was an idea that got her this job-vacation combination. She was the only girl in her class who was spending the summer in Hawaii. An idea helped save Miniki's flowers the day the cart broke down, the idea of submitting sketches with her story just might win her some recognition in Lili's contest, and her idea about Penni's being the Night Marcher might save Reef Royal from a serious blow. But that remained to be seen.

The thing that worried Vicki most about her talk with Lili was the accusation that she was afraid. This thought hadn't occurred to her before, but, of course, Lili was wrong. She had to be wrong. It was true that a switch from her parents' family to her own family left little room for independent adventure, but Vicki knew she would be acting out of love, not fear. She couldn't be guilty of the very thing she accused Mark of — of being afraid of responsibility.

Vicki sighed. Before she talked with Lili she had been ready to write, no, to call Greg and quickly accept his proposal of marriage. But Lili had a way of making a person think;

again Vicki's mind was muddled. Of course, she loved Greg. But . . . Well, she didn't have to make an immediate decision. It might be better to wait until after Lili announced the contest winner and the runners-up tomorrow. If Vicki were among the lucky ones named, the moment might be the turning point of her life.

In her room she slipped Greg's telegram under her pillow, then gathered the pages of her story. After inserting the best sketches in their proper places, she put the entire manuscript in a large manila envelope and started down the hallway to deliver it to Lili.

Chapter Fifteen

Vicki lay turning and squirming in bed long after everyone else had retired. Through her screened doorway she watched the shimmering silver moonlight gloss the green lawn and she heard the gossip of banyan leaves as the trade winds whispered in from the ocean. Rising from bed, she pulled the drapery across the doorway to shut out these distractions, but many minutes later she still lay sleepless.

When she closed her eyes, the words of Greg's telegram marched across the darkness of her mind, and Lili's harsh words rang in her ears like the roar of the high tide. *You're afraid! Afraid!*

Vicki finally got up and slipped out onto the *lanai* where she curled into a bamboo chair and considered the full import of Lili's accusation. Again she tried to tell herself that Lili was wrong. How could a stranger know so much about her? But the longer she sat there, the more the truth began to seep into her mind.

Her past life seemed to spin before her eyes, and she began to count the times she had depended on some impulsive action to cover up her self-doubt. In high school she'd plunged into extra-curricular activities when she'd been afraid she couldn't keep up with Verne scholastically. She'd impulsively dragged Greg to Fisherman's Wharf when fear of a premature proposal loomed in her mind. She'd dashed to accuse Lafe Yankton of plotting against Lili when she feared she had failed Reef Royal and her relatives. Considered in this way, her life seemed to fall into a pattern of impulsive acts designed to cover up her self-doubts.

Vicki sat arguing with herself in the darkness for another terrible hour before she finally gave in and admitted the unpleasant truth. Lili was right. She was afraid. Vicki knew she had made pretty much of a mess of things in Hawaii. She'd caused Reef Royal to lose customers by forcing Lili to move sooner than necessary. She'd made a bad choice of friends in Penni Pulianano, and she'd left herself open to failure by entering Lili's contest. And she had been about to accept Greg's proposal as a way out of her difficulties. Once she faced the truth, her next move became easier.

Fumbling her way to the desk, Vicki

snapped on the writing lamp and began a letter to Greg. The more she wrote the better she felt, and she knew Greg would agree with her decision to postpone wedding plans. Both of them wanted a marriage based on love, not on fear or on a desire for security.

Vicki didn't tell Greg of the contest winners to be announced the next afternoon, but she felt that writing this letter before the announcement was her first step toward independence. She would be cowardly to accept Greg's proposal after she lost the contest and heartless to reject it if she won. Greg deserved better than that; he deserved a wife who came to marriage not because she doubted she could do anything else with her life, but rather because she had proved herself in demanding fields and felt equal to the challenge marriage offered.

Vicki wrote a long, time-consuming letter. It was nearly morning when she signed it and sealed the envelope, but when she crawled into bed, she fell asleep immediately.

A persistent tapping on her door finally awakened Vicki the next morning. Rubbing the sleep from her eyes she glanced at her clock and realized that she'd missed the alarm — overslept again. What would Aunt Noel say!

"Who's there?" Vicki leaped out of bed and grabbed her robe.

"Aunt Noel, Vicki, may I come in?"

Vicki opened the door. "I overslept, Aunt Noel, but I'll work fast to make up for it."

"You needn't rush, Vicki." Aunt Noel smiled. "I forgot to tell you yesterday that we operate a relaxed Sunday schedule at Reef Royal. We serve mid-morning brunch which allows our employees and guests to attend church either before or after eating. Our only other meal is a buffet around four in the afternoon. Would you like to go to church with me now? You can help with the brunch when we return."

"That'll be fine, Aunt Noel." Vicki began making her bed. "What time will you leave?"

"Can you be ready in twenty minutes?"

"Sure thing." As soon as her aunt left the room, Vicki washed and dressed, and she reached the *lanai* just as her aunt drove the car into the driveway. Vicki slipped onto the front seat, and they visited on the brief ride to the church.

Vicki touched a crisp, red leaf on the beef-steak hedge which bordered the lush green lawn of the churchyard like a thick crimson ribbon, and she was so intent on admiring the flame-tipped branches of a Royal Poinciana tree that she stumbled over the doorsill to the old-fashioned, lava-rock church. Once inside she listened to the steeple bell call the worshipers to prayer, and at the same time she admired the rattan baskets of red anthurium and white ginger blossoms which decorated the altar. As she joined the hymn singing she knew that she had never attended a worship service in such beautiful surroundings. It was over all too soon.

"Where does Lili go to church?" Vicki asked as they walked to the car after the minister's closing benediction.

"She usually comes here with me," Aunt Noel answered. "But this morning she went to early church so she could spend the rest of the morning making final decisions about the contest entries."

When they returned to Reef Royal, Vicki changed her clothes and went to the kitchen where she sipped a glass of sweet guava juice before beginning her duties. As usual, the buffet looked almost too lovely to touch, but the guests did justice to their meal, leaving almost nothing on the table except the red and yellow hibiscus blossoms.

"Mark wants to see you out back when you're through working." Buzz whispered in Vicki's ear as he toted a tray of coffee cups to the kitchen.

Vicki had put their evening plans out of her mind until she absolutely had to consider them. Now that time was here. She stalled by helping herself to a wedge of papaya from the depleted buffet table.

"Mark wants to check your costume," Buzz whispered on a return trip to the dining area.

Vicki finished her hasty snack and dashed to the laundry room. She was in luck. Three of Lili's voluminous muumuus hung like limp balloons on the clothes line. Picking a yellow and orange one, Vicki found a stout length of cord and returned to her room for a pillow and one of Sue's floppy beach hats.

Just as she was trying to decide how she could get her burden across the hotel lawn to the jungle without being seen, Buzz appeared at her *lanai* carrying a shovel and pushing a red wheelbarrow covered with a tarp.

"In here, Vicki." He lifted the green canvas, and Vicki hid her costume from view. "Now if you'll carry the shovel and drag that hose along behind us, nobody will think a thing about our going toward the thicket. Everyone here is used to seeing me work in the yard."

Vicki followed Buzz's suggestion, and when they slipped onto the path leading into the jungle, they found Mark sitting under a breadfruit tree waiting for them. Buzz set the wheelbarrow beside a hibiscus bush and threw back the tarp, and Vicki held the muumuu up for Mark's inspection. Although she was eager to hear Mark's opinion of her get-up, she couldn't help noticing the exotic, full-blown growth that surrounded them, and she felt as if she were a midget viewing the world through a magnifying glass.

"Want me to slip this on?" Vicki asked as Mark examined the tent-like garment with a critical stare.

"Not now," Mark decided. "It looks okay. We'll hide it here behind this philodendron until tonight. Now, is everything all set? Buzz, did you talk to Penni?"

"Sure did." Buzz picked up a yellow plumeria blossom that had fallen to the ground and stuck it behind his ear. "I even paid him two dollars on my account to make my trip seem for real. You should have seen his face when I mentioned that Lili wasn't moving. Would you believe! He turned white as Lafe Yankton's suit."

"I'd believe," Vicki said. "But exactly what did he say?"

"Oh, he tried to let on that nothing was bothering him," Buzz said. "But I could tell he was upset. Whenever I make a payment on my surfboard, he always lets me take his special model out to catch a few waves. But not this time! He spouted large excuses — said he had a surfing lesson scheduled and that he was in a hurry. But when I walked off, he left the beach, and I saw him dash into a phone booth. I'll bet Lafe Yankton got a fast and frantic call."

"Let's hope so," Mark said.

"How about your camera, Buzz?" Vicki asked. "Is it working okay? You have plenty of film and flash bulbs?"

"Everything under control." Buzz grinned and gave a snappy salute.

"Buzz, you can hide behind the aerial roots of that small banyan." Mark pointed to the thick-trunked tree. "You should be able to get a flash shot from there. And Vicki, you stroll right along this path toward the ekoa thicket. In fact, stall in this vicinity if you have to. Pick some ekoa pods — anything. I'll hide behind these fern trees where the tangle of cereus vines is thickest. Both of you make noise but keep out of the way when the action starts. I want Penni, but I also want to give his friends plenty of room for escape. I can't handle all three at once."

"I'm no good at tackling, but I'll go for

help if the opposition looks too tough," Vicki said.

"That's unlikely," Mark said. "I know Penni's friends. If my guess is right, they'll zoom off like jets when they discover we're on to them. Right now we'd better get back to the hotel before we're missed."

"Buzz," Vicki said. "Have you thought of some way to keep Lili from taking her evening walk?"

"Sure," Buzz answered. "She always starts her stroll around seven-thirty, so I'll go to her room about seven-twenty and ask about some point of Hawaiian history, maybe something concerning the Waimea canyon on Kauai. I've done this before. Lili has lots of reference books, and she always gets them right when I ask. Then I'll tell her the information is for a guest who's taking an early morning tour and who always retires early. I'll ask her to leave the information at the desk before eight-thirty tonight. Anyway, when she's busy looking up this history of the canyon, I'll excuse myself and join you."

"Sounds all right," Vicki agreed. "Good thing Lili's so obliging."

"If that doesn't work out, I'll detain her by talking to her," Buzz promised. "I'll stash my camera by the banyan earlier in the evening, then all I'll have to do is sprint out here and go into hiding."

"We'd better slip back to the hotel," Vicki suggested. "Mark, you go first. We'll give you five minutes, then we'll follow with the wheelbarrow."

When they were safely out of the jungle, Vicki reported to the kitchen to see if she could be of any help. Aunt Noel put her to work, and Vicki was glad that her duties allowed no moments for worrying about the evening ahead or for fretting the outcome of Lili's contest. Vicki carried dishes, platters of cold cuts, and bowls of fruits between the kitchen and dining areas until all was in readiness for the guests.

The late-afternoon buffet was the most leisurely meal Vicki had witnessed at Reef Royal. The patrons lingered over their dessert, then chatted while they enjoyed an extra cup of coffee or glass of iced tea. Vicki tried to hide her impatience, but before everyone had left the dining room and kitchen, it was almost time for Lili to announce her contest winners, and there was no time to change clothes or freshen up. Vicki was so tense and nervous that she almost wished she hadn't entered the event.

Most of the guests had drifted straight from the dining area to the front lobby where Buzz and Mark had set up extra folding chairs, and Vicki slipped to the rear of the noisy group. By standing behind the guests she was inconspicuous, yet she was in a position to see and hear all that happened.

When Lili appeared, all chatter ceased and the hush was like the silence between a benediction and a postlude; no one moved or even whispered. Lili wore an ankle-length green satin dress with a flowing train that swept the floor behind her. If she had mounted a diamond-studded tiara on her silver hair, she truly would have looked the part of a queen at court.

Lili's smile was her greeting to the crowd, but Vicki could tell that it was a bittersweet smile of sadness. Although her great dignity precluded any sentiment, she spoke briefly of her regret at leaving Reef Royal, then as was her custom, she came right to the point of her speech.

"The winning entry in this year's creative writing contest is a short story submitted by . . ." Lili paused, and Vicki felt her heart pounding like the beating surf. "Submitted by Holly Hastings."

The guests gave Holly a standing ovation, and she stepped forward, pink-faced and excited, to accept the coveted award Lili held toward her. Although Vicki hadn't really expected to win, her throat ached until she could hardly swallow or breathe.

What had made her think she could write! Just because she could thrill a few neighborhood children with bed-time stories, just because she had a journal full of descriptions and impressions! It wasn't enough. She'd just let herself in for a big disappointment.

The crowd quieted once again as Lili began reading the names of the persons whose stories would appear in the year's anthology. Vicki waited tense, yet hopeful, as Lili called out nine names, then already trying to adjust to defeat, she could hardly believe she'd heard correctly when her own name sounded above the murmur of the crowd.

"*The Boy Who Lost A Giraffe* by Vicki Foster." Lili smiled as she spoke, and Vicki wanted to rush to her, to thank her. But the crowd blocked her way, and everyone broke into a roar of chatter and congratulations.

Her story in print! Vicki felt as if she were a balloon filled with gas and about to float to the sky. It was all she could do to murmur politely to the guests as they offered her their best wishes. When at last the crowd began to thin out, Vicki rushed to congratulate Holly. They both looked around for Lili, but she had disappeared from the scene.

Only now after the contest was over did Vicki realize how much she had wanted to win. As she went to her room, tears of happiness stung her eyes, and she felt a growing gratitude toward Lili who had urged her to enter the competition in the first place, Lili who had preached the value of ideas. Yes, the same Lili who had caused her to bristle like a porcupine when she'd told her she was afraid to face life on her own.

Before Vicki could sort out her feelings, a knock sounded on her door and when she answered, Buzz handed her a folded slip of paper, then hurried away. She opened the message.

"Vicki,
Congratulations! I see a writing career ahead of you if you're willing to work for it. Lili asked me to tell you to come to her room, but do that later. Right now, come down to earth. The real contest is about to begin.

Mark"

Vicki stared dreamily at the note. She

wondered what Lili wanted to see her about, but her curiosity was dulled by Mark's signature on the note. Mark had congratulated her! Mark!

Chapter Sixteen

Vicki tried to relax, tried to forget the writing competition and to concentrate on the problem at hand. She sprawled across her bed staring at the ceiling and going over their plans in her mind until Buzz slipped onto her *lanai* and scratched at the screen.

"Let's go, Vicki." Buzz whispered, but Vicki caught the urgency in his words and felt a cypher of hollowness expand in the pit of her stomach. Her idea for an illustrated story had rated in Lili's writing contest, but Vicki had creeping doubts about the success of this other thought. How she wished she had never mentioned this crazy scheme!

Buzz would do anything for Reef Royal, but she knew Mark was going along with her ideas only as a last effort — a final attempt to help Lili and his mother. And right now she shared all of Mark's misgivings. What if the Marchers didn't appear? Or worse, what if they did appear and Mark was injured in his attempt to tackle Penni?

Or what if the strange marchers weren't Penni and his friends?

"Vicki! Come on!" Buzz glanced over the hotel grounds, then adjusted the camera slung around his neck. "There's no one in sight, Lili's busy hunting information about the canyon, and if we're careful we can make it to the jungle without being seen."

"Okay, Buzz, let's go." Vicki trailed Buzz as if they were playing follow the leader — under the banyan tree, past the orchid beds, and at last through the hibiscus hedge and into the jungle. Like a caged animal Mark was pacing nervously back and forth in the red dust of the narrow path, and when they appeared he hurried toward them.

"It's about time! Thought you two were going to desert at the last minute. Get into costume, Vicki. We've no time to spare."

After tying the pillow around her middle, Vicki slipped Lili's muumuu on over her regular clothes, jammed the straw beach hat on her head, and tucked her hair out of sight.

"Get all those buttons fastened and keep your head down," Mark warned. "You'll pass for Lili easily enough if you keep your face in the shadows."

Vicki jerked the floppy hat brim lower onto her forehead.

"Buzz, let's vanish," Mark said. "If Penni's going to show, it'll be soon. Vicki, you start walking. Slowly. Stay as close to my hiding place as you can."

Vicki's legs felt wobbly as rubber bands, but she made herself keep moving. As soon as Mark and Buzz hid, she felt as if she had been abandoned, but as minutes passed with no action she began to relax.

The trade wind carried the honeyed fragrance of ginger, but as she inhaled deeply Vicki heard a foreboding buzzing. Peering through the dusk, she spotted bees droning over some fallen mangoes. Angling off the path, Vicki picked up one of the orange-red fruits, polished it on the front of Lili's muumuu, and bit through the protecting skin into sweet, firm flesh.

Although she wasn't hungry, the peach-like flavor of the fruit distracted her mind from the terrible waiting, and she considered her future as she walked along. Vicki had no idea of how long she thought about all her problems and choices, but when she finally discarded the mango seed and was about to stoop to wipe her hands on the grass, Buzz sprang from his hiding place and jerked her thoughts back to the present.

"It's Lili!" Buzz thrust his camera into Vicki's hands. "I just heard her call to

Mother from the back *lanai*. She must have finished her research sooner than I thought she would, and she's probably headed this way."

"What'll we do?" Vicki asked. "We can't have her out here now."

"I'll cut through the brush to our left and head her off," Buzz said as he began to run. "I'll think of something."

"Better make it good," Mark called after him.

As Vicki glanced at the camera in her hands, she realized that Buzz probably wouldn't get back to take any pictures. They would be lucky if he managed to sidetrack Lili this second time. Did Mark know how to use the camera? There was no opportunity to ask him now. Vicki ducked her head, hat and all, through the brown leather loop, then tucked the camera out of sight under the muumuu as she continued her intense walking. Who would appear first, the phony Night Marchers or Lili? Or maybe no one at all would come. The minutes dragged on and on.

A blood-red moon rested on the horizon like a danger signal; then, as it rose higher into the sky, it changed from pink to silver-gray. Vicki was beginning to think that Penni had ignored Buzz's information about Lili's not moving when she saw a faint flicker of light dancing behind the slender trunks of the royal palms. She wished she could alert Mark, but a telltale movement from behind the cereus vines told her that he too had seen the light.

Forcing herself to keep walking, Vicki strained to see more of the lights, and presently three forms stepped into the tropical moonlight of a small clearing. Torch flames wavered, and Vicki held her breath. Their faces hidden in shadows, the yellow-caped figures with their crested helmets and tall feather staves formed a scene of ancient splendor.

In that moment Vicki forgot fear and knew only empathy with Lili Lanuoka. Here in this hushed place of tropical island beauty it was easy to understand how a person with Lili's background might come to believe that she was encountering spirits of the past, *alii* from another world.

But Vicki had no time for such reverie. The tallest of the three figures stepped toward her.

"Lili Lanuoka."

Although she recognized Penni Pulianano's velvet-smooth voice, Vicki kept her face hidden and tried to brace for whatever might happen next.

"Lili Lanuoka! Listen! Your ancestor speaks. This land is *kapu!* You must move toward the mountains. You must move to the property of Lafe Yankton. Yes, you must live at Hale Maile and never again disturb our marches."

Although she had known exactly what was going to happen, Vicki gasped as Mark sprang from behind the cereus vines with a roaring yell and a running tackle. Penni thudded to the ground, but instead of running, his two companions stood frozen with surprise.

What if they stood firm? What if they realized that Mark was no match for the three of them? Vicki thought fast. Pulling Buzz's camera from under her muumuu she aimed in the general direction of the two accomplices and snapped the shutter. She had closed her own eyes in anticipation of the blinding glare from the flash bulb, and when she opened them she saw that the two light-blinded impostors had dropped their torches and were fleeing in fright.

While Vicki scrambled to retrieve the flaming sticks before they ignited a brush fire, Mark sat on Penni's middle and pinned his arms to the ground.

"Let me up!" Penni struggled for a moment, then relaxed as he realized that Mark had him in a painful position.

"Why'd you do it?" Mark asked. "What's the idea of trying to scare an old lady?"

"Lafe Yankton," Penni gasped. "Lafe Yankton. His idea."

"Suppose you come to Reef Royal and tell that story to Lili Lanuoka." Mark clamped Penni's arm behind his back with a grip firm enough to show that his suggestion was really an order, and Vicki lighted their way back to the hotel with the burning torches.

Aunt Noel met them on the back lawn with Lili and Buzz close behind her. The two ladies stopped, speechless, and Vicki had to smile as she imagined the picture they must present — she in an outsize muu-muu carrying three glowing torches, Penni in his awe-inspiring costume of ancient Hawaii, and Mark commanding the entire situation.

"Shades of Lono!" Aunt Noel cried.

"It's one of the Night Marchers," Lili said in a hushed voice.

"It's a hoax, Lili. A trick. This is Penni Pulianano, a beach boy from Waikiki." Vicki looked to Mark for confirmation of her statements.

"Tell her." Mark nudged Penni.

"It's true," Penni said. "Lafe Yankton

hired me to persuade you to move to his place so he'd have your writers' colony in residence at Hale Maile. What are you going to do to me? I wasn't alone in this, you know."

"Let him go," Lili said to Mark.

"Let him go?" Mark, Buzz, and Vicki asked in chorus.

"Yes," Lili said. "I never want to see him again. I'll deal with Lafe Yankton personally."

Mark released his grip on Penni, and as the boy tried to make a dignified exit from Reef Royal, he only succeeded in looking more foolish than ever in his outlandish costume.

"Buzz," Aunt Noel said. "For heaven's sake, do something with those torches Vicki is carrying before they set the whole place on fire. And the rest of you, come. Let's all go to my room and talk this over."

Buzz took the torches and by the time they were settled inside the hotel he rejoined them. Vicki told Lili that she had spent an evening with Penni and had thus suspected it was he who tried to trick her.

"I'm afraid we've ruined your muumuu, Lili," Mark said. "It's torn in front, and there're pin-point burns all over it from the sparking torches."

213

"I'm glad," Lili replied.

"Glad?" Aunt Noel questioned.

"Glad that it's only a muumuu that's ruined and not the rest of my life. I was silly and stubborn to regress back to believing in Night Marchers, and I suppose you Fosters think me a complete fool."

"Of course not, Lili," Aunt Noel said. "We're only glad that we're going to continue to have you with us. Everyone stay right here; I'm going to perk some coffee to soothe our shattered nerves."

"Vicki, I understand now why you didn't come to my apartment after the contest announcements as I asked you to do. You were no doubt too busy with your scheme for this evening."

Vicki nodded. "Forgive me, Lili. I did want to give you my personal thanks for including my story in the anthology, but this other business had to be finished. You'll never know how glad I am that you are staying on at Reef Royal, nor how proud I am to have won your approval of my writing. This whole affair has given me a feeling of confidence that's beyond description."

"I wanted to talk to you about your writing," Lili said. "It shows talent and promise, and I have an offer to make to you if it's not too late. I can get you a part-time job as typist at the *Gazette*. It's not much of a job, but it would keep you moving in a journalistic world. There's no better place for an observant person who wants to write."

"I'm sorry, Lili, but I have to refuse," Vicki said.

"Vicki." Mark jumped up. "Don't be a dope. That's a good offer, and you're foolish to turn it down."

"I think that perhaps Vicki has a better offer from a young man on the mainland." Lili smiled sadly at Mark.

"While I was waiting for the Night Marchers to appear, I had lots of time to think about many things," Vicki said. "I don't plan to be married for a long, long time, Lili. I've decided to take a chance on myself." Vicki turned as Aunt Noel came back into the room carrying a silver tray of coffee.

"Aunt Noel, I'd like to go on working here at Reef Royal for as long as you'll have me. Sue'll be staying on the mainland, and Mark's told me you'll need someone to replace her in the fall."

"Why, of course, we can use you if you care to stay," Aunt Noel replied.

"I think I can do my hotel work and also enroll in some afternoon university classes. I may not make straight 'A's' but I'll consider myself successful if I learn things that will help me advance as a writer. And, Lili, if you'll read and criticize some more stories that I intend to write, I'll really be grateful."

Lili nodded, but before anyone could speak, there was confusion in the lobby, and Buzz went to investigate. Returning immediately, he announced that Lafe Yankton wished to see Mrs. Foster.

"Now, the rest of you stay here," Aunt Noel said. "I'll deal with Lafe."

"I have a few things to say to him myself." Lili rose, and Buzz followed them from the room.

"You were great tonight, Mark," Vicki said when they were alone. "I was proud of you."

"The feeling is mutual." Mark looked at Vicki, then lowered his eyes. "You're quite a kid, Vicki."

"Me?" Vicki laughed. "It was just a crazy scheme that happened to work out well."

"I'm not talking about our experience with Penni," Mark said. "I'm impressed by anyone who's willing to face life with nothing backing them but their own inner resources. I thought for a while that you were going to give up, to take the easy way out, but you fooled me. Turning down

Greg's proposal is probably one of the bravest things you'll ever do. That took real courage, Vicki."

Vicki blushed at Mark's unexpected praise, and she considered his words thoughtfully before she answered. "Mark, I owe you an apology."

"What for?" her cousin asked.

"Because when you said you wanted time to think and loaf, I thought that you were afraid — afraid to face the responsibility of managing Reef Royal. Because I was afraid, I thought you were, too. But that was a wrong impression, wasn't it? You hate being thrown into this hotel work *because* of the security it offers, don't you? You resent missing the opportunity to — well — to be yourself, to see if you can make it on your own."

"I suppose that's right in a way," Mark admitted. "Now that you've said it out loud in plain words, it seems rather simple. I've been behaving like a spoiled child fretting for a lollipop that's out of reach."

"But you're no spoiled child, Mark. I don't blame you for being resentful, now that I understand your point of view. I wish there were something I could do to help."

"Vicki, you've already helped by straightening out some of my mixed-up thinking. Oh, I'm not walking out on Reef Royal — I still have a duty here. I may not always radiate sweetness and light, but I'm going to try to be pleasant while I stick it out as hotel manager for a couple more years until Buzz can begin to take over. Then I'll cut out on my own."

"Buzz loves Reef Royal. He can't wait to step in, but you'll be twenty-two by then, Mark."

"The perfect age for a great adventure!" Mark grinned, and for the first time Vicki saw the grin reach clear to his eyes.

Later that night, Vicki crawled into bed with her mind bursting with all sorts of thoughts. She was excited, but she didn't make the mistake of interpreting the excitement as fear. It was excess energy — energy to be called up and used as needed. Now that she had a worthy goal in mind, she didn't feel as if she was running away from San Francisco. Her plans for the coming months were based on her high hope that an education, plus hard work, plus a few ideas, would add up to success. Somehow she knew that even her parents would approve of her decision.

Vicki felt that she had lived a decade in the past week, but she knew that any calendar would assure her that she was still only eighteen. *I may never be a great writer,* she thought, *but it's a goal to try for. The least I can do is to live independently long enough to find out where my strength is.* It suddenly occurred to her that she and Mark were again at odds — she was sure that eighteen was the most absolutely perfect age for a great adventure.

We hope you have enjoyed this Large Print book. Other Thorndike, Wheeler or Chivers Press Large Print books are available at your library or directly from the publishers.

For more information about current and upcoming titles, please call or write, without obligation, to:

Publisher
Thorndike Press
295 Kennedy Memorial Drive
Waterville, ME 04901
Tel. (800) 223-1244

Or visit our Web site at:
www.gale.com/thorndike
www.gale.com/wheeler

OR

Chivers Large Print
published by BBC Audiobooks Ltd
St James House, The Square
Lower Bristol Road
Bath BA2 3SB
England
Tel. +44(0) 800 136919
email: bbcaudiobooks@bbc.co.uk
www.bbcaudiobooks.co.uk

All our Large Print titles are designed for easy reading, and all our books are made to last.

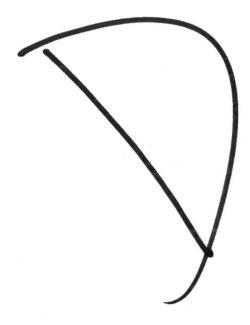